DAWN OF AFFINITY

V. J. DEANES

CHAPTER 1

Kalan Mars remained composed. A few of the seniors surrounded him as he walked alone behind the high school in Hadley's Crossing over the lunch hour. The older boys ignored Kalan's remark about wanting to be left alone. They sought him out to establish territory, as a rite of passage to determine his place in their small world.

When Gerald Huff's demand for Kalan to listen to him met with defiance he pushed Kalan to the ground. Kalan stood up and dusted himself off.

"Do you always pick on freshman to look tough in front of your girlfriends?" Kalan asked as he pointed to the other boys in Huff's gang.

Huff was annoyed. "Watch your tongue lad," he remarked. "Or, I'll have to rip it out." He started to walk in a circle around Kalan.

Kalan pointed to his crotch. "My fly is up. If I want any tongue wagging from you it will be down."

The small crowd that had gathered to watch the commotion became silent.

Huff lunged at Kalan, as if to throw a punch. Kalan didn't flinch.

"Tough guy," Kalan remarked. "Take your phone out of pocket. Dial 911. Call yourself an ambulance. Then throw a real punch."

Huff took the bait and went into a rage. Moments later he lay beaten and bloodied on the ground. Kalan landed a couple of extra blows for good measure. When Kalan stood up to walk away Huff reached for one of his legs. Kalan turned and kicked him hard in the ribs. Huff rolled over moaning in pain. Kalan had sent the message: I'm not afraid of anyone and I'll prove it to you.

Rick Sawyer and Doug Wilson returned from one of the lunch places down the road, closer into town. They caught up with Kalan a few moments after he handed Huff a dose of small-town schoolyard justice.

"Word has it that Huff is in hospital on life support," Rick said, as he pointed to a text message on his phone.

"That's what he deserves," Doug added. "No one has ever thrashed Gerald Huff like that before."

"Good job Kalan," Rick remarked. "Now all of your friends will be targets for life."

Kalan took exception to Rick's assessment of the situation. "I guess you would prefer to be Huff's slave."

Rick was silent.

"I had to put Huff in his place. Otherwise, I would just be another beaten down dweeb around here."

"He'll come back for retribution," Rick replied.

"So let him," said Kalan. "What are you afraid of?"

"Are you crazy?" Rick asked.

"Wake up Rick," Kalan remarked. "Hadley's Crossing is one big pecking order. Everyone in this town fits into their own little slot, in case you hadn't noticed. Doesn't matter how old they are, or how long they have lived here. This place is my ticket out," Kalan said as he pointed to the school. "No one is getting in my way."

"You're turning into an angry young man," Doug remarked. "Full of angst. Driven to rid the world of whatever you think is wrong with it. Amen to that."

"You see Rick," Kalan remarked. "Doug sees the situation for what it is."

"Yes, I do see the situation for what it is," Doug noted. "Picking fights in a place where everyone knows each other won't get you too far. Word spreads fast. Pretty soon we'll all get dragged into this mess. It won't be long until you are an outcast."

"That's what I'm talking about," said Rick. "Maybe there's something to be said for fitting into the fabric of small town life after all."

"That comment certainly wins the prize for the lamest remark of the hour," said Devon Granger who had walked up behind Rick and Doug as they gave Kalan a hard time.

"Who are you?" Rick asked as he turned around.

"The alien from the big city," Devon replied. "Too bad I missed the excitement. I would have landed a few on Huff if you needed me to."

Kalan took a few moments to introduce Devon to his life-long friends from the neighborhood.

"Devon is new here. Met him in English class. What has it been, almost three weeks since you moved to Hadley's Crossing?"

"Feels more like three months."

"He has come to search for excitement in our town."

"Stranded here by my parents' desire for a slower pace is more like it," Devon said.

Rick and Doug were not sure what to make of the newcomer. The untucked blue and white striped shirt, red pants, and red running shoes gave him an appearance that was far from the small-town standard issue blue denim look. Added to his self-confident swagger was an aura of impatience as if Devon needed life to move at a faster pace than it ever could in Hadley's Crossing.

Rick's and Doug's fears about Gerald Huff seemed to matter even less to Devon than to Kalan. Where Kalan's tenacity was motivated by fairness and holding his ground, Devon's apparent willingness to take out a thug like Huff was driven purely by the sport of it. That attitude was like fresh air for Kalan. It drove him to know more about Devon.

"Well boys that was an amusing lunch break," said Rick. "I can't wait to see what fun we have after school today."

"Are you still nervous?" Kalan asked. "Nothing is going to happen."

The school day ended with Huff staring down Kalan and his friends as they left for home. Kalan's confident prediction held up. Huff muttered something before walking away in the opposite direction.

"What did I tell you, lads?" Kalan remarked. "The beast has been tamed."

The four boys walked a few blocks to the corner store.

"See you tomorrow," Rick and Doug said as they turned onto the street that led to their homes. Kalan and Devon had further to walk.

"Why did your parents come to Hadley's Crossing?" Kalan asked Devon. "They could have gone to any small town."

"I still haven't figured it out. Maybe they chose this town because of the peace and quiet. Closer to the outdoors," he remarked, pointing to the hills off in the distance. "They seem happy. What about your folks?"

"Lived here forever," Kalan answered. "High school sweethearts who never left."

The boys walked down 6th Street, happily chatting about the things that interest fourteen-year-olds. A light breeze gently rustled the leaves of the old trees that towered above the sidewalk that led through the oldest neighborhood in the town. Devon's appearance garnered looks of curiosity from people relaxing on the magnificent porches of the historic old brick homes.

"Getting used to everyone knowing everyone else's business?" Kalan asked.

"I'm too new around here to know much about that," Devon said. "I have heard something of the stories about how some families banded together to force other people to leave."

"Two kinds of people live in Hadley's Crossing, far as I can tell," Kalan remarked. "One kind has this unspoken bond. One kind never gets it. I can't explain."

"Which kind are you?" Devon asked.

"Don't really know," Kalan replied as he shrugged his shoulders.

"What about your parents?"

"I think my folks are the kind with the bond," Kalan answered.

"Ever think about what you're going to do when you finish school here?" Devon asked.

"No firm plans yet. Guess I'll have to start thinking about that soon," Kalan answered. "I know that I can't stay here my whole life. I will need to get away, to find some real action."

CHAPTER 2

9 years later in 2029

"Step forward," the mechanized voice requested. The nerdy looking man did as he was told. He knew the drill. Stand straight. No expression. Look forward. Relax.

"Technician. First class. Norman Bustafo you are cleared for entry. Proceed to assembly room fifteen."

"Bustafo. I should have guessed."

"What's that supposed to mean, MacGregor?"

"This job needs a real pro. Good to see that you decided to take it. I thought you packed this kind of work in a few years ago."

"I did," Bustafo replied. "The paycheck for this gig convinced me to spend a day or two away from my place by the ocean."

"We haven't worked a job together for, what, at least ten years?"

"Let's go for a beer and catch up before getting started on this. It's good to see you again."

"Time pressure is too tight," MacGregor confirmed. "Beer will have to wait until we're done. Trust me, we'll need an entire case. Come with me."

Bustafo followed MacGregor with interest. MacGregor pulled back a screen. "This is the one we need you to program." A human-form robot lay on an operating table. Its eyes stared lifelessly towards the ceiling.

"Is she ever hot," said Bustafo.

"It, not she," MacGregor corrected sternly.

"We haven't even started and you're already freaked out," Bustafo quipped.

"This one is dangerous," MacGregor said. "Even by my standards."

Bustafo was more inclined to take the situation seriously. "Why is that?"

8

"You might not have been given all of the facts about this one. It has self-destruct capabilities. When we begin the actuation sequence..."

"Slow down," Bustafo requested. "This is a suicide machine. Is that what you are saying? 'Cause if it is, I'm out. I don't do this kind of..."

"Calm down," MacGregor insisted. "It's not what you think."

"Only espionage-class robots can have that capability," Bustafo replied.

"This robot is espionage-class," MacGregor replied.

"Self-destruct capabilities and assassin programming? So how come I was told this gig was to program a robot to act as if it was a medical doctor?"

"You should buff up on the regulations," MacGregor replied. "After the fiasco with the thousand imposters, autonomous robots can have assassination and self-destruct capabilities, but only with primary classifications as either spies or spy hunters. They can also have secondary classifications as first responders to high-risk situations, or as medical doctors engaged in certain types of research."

"You're saying this machine is an autonomous spy first and a doctor second?" Bustafo questioned.

"Something like that," MacGregor replied. "It has pre-set personality and thought process programs required for espionage. It needs additional programming, specifically pertaining to human enhancement. It must behave as a medical professional while concealing that it is a spy hunter."

"If this thing goes haywire I just need to know that it's not coming back on my head," Bustafo said.

"You're covered in that regard," MacGregor confirmed. "All risks have been assumed by the buyer. That's the only way the permit was granted."

"Someone seems to have insisted that I get onto this project," Bustafo mentioned. "Know much about that?"

"You worked on the system architecture that was used to program the behavior characteristics of the thousand imposters," MacGregor remarked. "That set the baseline for adaptive machine learning in autonomous humanoids to live with humans and to learn from them. We need you to make this robot behave like a scientist."

"This robot is different," Bustafo countered. "The imposters, as they are now known, were entirely biological. Identical to humans in almost every way. Their brains were connected to memory and microprocessor implants that required intermittent updates, to provide the situational context of being an adult. The imposters, as you call them, were designed with programming for basic human functions, including a full lifespan. The learning program layer that I worked on let them adapt to their social surroundings on an open-ended basis."

"You must know what really happened to the imposters," MacGregor remarked. "It is still top secret."

"The truth is that a thousand autonomous manufactured human replicas were introduced into society for the purpose of observing how well they fit in with humans. Think about it. Once they were switched on they instantly became adults, between twenty and thirty years old. They were a success. You couldn't tell them apart from humans. They had jobs. Some were parents. Two of them became criminals. Panic ensued when the public learned that two androids broke the law. Anti-robot, anti-android, anti-clone rhetoric sparked fear. Most of the imposters were tracked down, then switched off."

"You think that it was improper to hunt them down?"

"It was unnecessary," Bustafo replied. "They were no more of a danger to society than you or me. Unlike this one," he said while pointing to the robot on the operating table.

"I see your point," MacGregor noted.

"Tell me more about this beauty," Bustafo requested.

"This one is fully autonomous. It will be perceived as a normal human being by the people it encounters. In reality, it will only interact with a small number of humans in settings that will be highly controlled. That was also a condition in the permit."

"This robot is a killer. It needs to have a termination date," Bustafo said. "Lifespan length of this robot needs to be factored into the programming."

"This robot, like the imposters, has no fixed lifespan," MacGregor replied.

"You should know that there is a high probability of personality disruption," Bustafo stated.

"Go on," MacGregor encouraged.

"An autonomous robot with a human lifespan that also has a near-term death objective will be conflicted. It will become accustomed to a consciousness similar to humans. The knowledge that it may need to terminate will confuse it. On the one hand, it will mimic human instincts for survival and longevity. On the other hand, it will be programmed to terminate itself under certain conditions. It could exhibit behaviors that are antisocial. It will be aggressive and confrontational with humans. Perhaps it will even exhibit symptoms of depression and psychosis, during times when it must reconcile whether or not to terminate."

"We can live with that risk," MacGregor confirmed.

"Are you sure? You said something about preset spy programming. I question whether it understands basic human values and the choices that we make based on those values."

"What are you saying?

"A killing machine that has no sense of right and wrong," Bustafo replied. "This must be one hell of a mission."

MacGregor didn't respond.

"Where are you sending it?"

"You aren't supposed to know that."

"It's probably better that way," Bustafo remarked.

"What I can tell you," MacGregor continued, "is that this robot will watch over scientists who are on the leading edge of genetic research. To make sure that secrets are not stolen."

"Where do we start?"

"We need you to upload the reference points on which the robot will build its scientific knowledge," MacGregor replied.

"What's up with the port? File transfer and wireless together?"

"I admit it is somewhat dated," MacGregor conceded. He touched a mole on one side of the robot's head and pulled it back to reveal a tiny FTP port. "We want all of the reference files loaded directly into memory."

"Then what happens?"

"This robot has the learning layer from one of the imposters."

"Where did you get that from?" Bustafo asked.

"From one of the imposters that was decommissioned," MacGregor answered.

"Do you have the number?"

"Unit one hundred and fifty one."

Bustafo thought for a moment. "She's the one that became a nurse if memory serves me correctly."

"Precisely. She had the closest behavior patterns to those required by this robot. Her learning algorithms may be dated, but we know they work." MacGregor remarked.

"Yes, we do," Bustafo reaffirmed.

"Before we start," MacGregor noted, "what happened to those who let the imposters loose? I understood that the original plan was for the robots to be contained in a small town somewhere, not in a city."

"Beats me," Bustafo replied. "Don't forget that the riots and demonstrations protesting the discontinued use of historical references for major cities happened at the same time," Bustafo noted. "Fracturing of society into Red Zones and Blue Zones. The emergence of Haven Cities. The onset of bombings and terror attacks in Red Zones. People had bigger things to deal with than those officials who, with permission and encouragement, let the imposters free into the general population."

MacGregor walked around the robot to a set of computers.

"We'll start by loading some archival information that documents important events in the science of human enhancement. This will establish a simple baseline of knowledge. I will upload modern databases where relevant information on human enhancement is stored today. Once it becomes active, assuming the start sequence doesn't initiate the self-destruct routines, you and I will observe how it builds on the baseline knowledge. Then we will observe it in the virtual reality simulator, to see how it responds to test scenarios." Bustafo opened his tablet computer and began transferring knowledge to the robot.

"Reports of cloning human embryos first appeared back in 2001," said Bustafo.

"Those reports were never proven," MacGregor replied.

"Without confirmation that replicating humans has ever been common practice, the subject will always be presented as speculation by those who control the practice of creating humans in a lab," Bustafo noted.

"Let the machine determine if that is fact or fiction," MacGregor requested.

"Stories about laboratories dedicated to harvesting spare organs from human replicas surfaced in 2010."

"Were those laboratories located in hidden government bases?" MacGregor asked. "The same bases where armies of clone soldiers lived before they went into military service?"

Bustafo shook his head. "From 2013 through 2017 the scientific literature documented several advances that I think your robot needs to understand. Start with human cloning, where DNA was successfully transferred from an adult cell into an unfertilized egg after the original DNA had been removed."

"Go on," MacGregor requested.

"Predictions that artificial human organs would be farmed as an alternative to using animals to test the effects of chemicals and drugs surfaced soon after. A timeline for ectogenesis, or pregnancy that takes place in an artificial environment, was proposed next. Experiments, where animals were grown in artificial wombs, were successful a couple of years later."

MacGregor watched with interest as Bustafo chose what information to upload to the robot.

"Harvesting individual human organs that were grown in dedicated reactors was considered a viable means to satisfy the demand for life-saving transplants. Scientists then demonstrated that 3D printed human cartilage grew successfully in test mice."

"A baby was born from a procedure that combined DNA from three people. Permission to use mitochondrial transfer for in-vitro fertilization to create babies from three people was granted as well."

"Here is something your robot should take note of," Bustafo remarked. "Leaders of national intelligence agencies around the world proclaimed that genome editing increases the risk of creating potentially harmful biological agents."

MacGregor listened even more keenly.

"Gene editing, where DNA was modified in the genome of an organism to produce targeted mutations was awarded scientific breakthrough of the year. This technique was studied to switch off specific genes that control the development of embryos. Scientists then successfully edited embryos to remove faulty DNA that causes heart disease to be hereditary."

"Editing genes inside a human body to permanently change a person's DNA, in an attempt to fight an incurable disease, was demonstrated right around the time that the first human-form female robot was granted rights of citizenship."

"Now for the finale," Bustafo remarked. "The design of a nano-machine, built with DNA, that could change shape in response to external stimuli, such as a digital signal, was proposed just before scientists demonstrated that a movie could be encoded into living cells and subsequently retrieved at will. Imagine neurons as biological recording devices."

MacGregor watched as Bustafo organized his source files then uploaded them through the FTP port. "That's it?" he asked. "Only a few reference points. Will that be enough?"

"Will it be enough? That depends on your machine," Bustafo replied. "With the system architecture in this robot, I would be shocked if it couldn't come up to an expert level of understanding of this subject matter within a couple of hours."

MacGregor looked skeptical.

"All your machine needs are the basics and some context," Bustafo remarked. "Capability to edit human genetics. Approval for babies to be born with modified genes. Reproducing mammals in artificial wombs. The potential threats that artificial humans pose. Granting human-form robots rights of citizenship. Storage of digital information in DNA. Using DNA as a digital switch from one state to another based on external stimuli."

"You make it sound simple," MacGregor remarked.

"Why are you surprised?" Bustafo asked. "The information I uploaded is old news. Creating purpose-built humans with minds that connect to the Internet has to happen sooner or later. That thought never occurred to you?"

XXXX

The newest member of the Society for the Elimination of Artificial People immediately caught the attention of those in charge. The militant young man promised to demonstrate an intriguing method for determining whether a person had a double that they did not know of. It could radically alter the society's effectiveness if used wisely. In the wrong hands, it could lead to the society's ruin, which is why the founder arranged an urgent meeting with the young inventor.

"Are you Stone?"

"Have a seat Mister Gedder," Stone gestured.

"Why are you afraid to use my invention?" the younger man asked.

"We recruited you into our society after we watched you for a while. You know someone who we need to know," Stone replied. "Besides, you seem dedicated to our cause. A little prone to extremist behavior, but dedicated. We had no idea that you would bring us anything more."

"That doesn't answer my question."

"You must not mix up what some of the members have told you with my interests," Stone replied. "Their fears are well-founded, but not insurmountable. Show me how it works."

The young man set up his demonstration on the table. A tablet computer and mobile phone automatically searched social media sites, while simultaneously running a facial recognition program using a single still photographic image as a reference. If the software matched a face from an Internet search to the face in a still image, it searched for a mobile phone number. It also hacked into local area networks to access video footage and audio files, to verify names and whether the pair might be related. The underlying assumption, Vern Gedder explained, was that the people who resembled those in the still photographs were clones.

The algorithms could analyze demographics, once the software had uncovered a few hundred combinations of people who looked identical and yet appeared to have no relationship to one another. Even Stone was surprised to find that most of the individuals labeled as potential clones by Vern's software lived in only three communities; Foxtown, Hadley's Crossing and Polby.

"Why are you afraid to confront them?" Vern asked.

"I am impressed with what you showed me," Stone remarked. "I admire your tenacity. Don't confuse fear with caution, or discretion with inaction."

The young man listened carefully.

"Our society works behind the scenes, as you must already know. We need to keep a low profile. The relationships that our older members cultivate with like-minded doctors and scientists supply an invaluable amount of knowledge about those who would attempt to clone humans and deploy human-form robots. Scientists who abide by the law depend on us to protect their identities. They count on us to work with authorities to bring the ones who seek to modify the human form to justice."

"Younger associates in our society are asked to befriend younger family members and friends of the scientists, to bring us even more information. It may seem like inaction to you, but we cast a ubiquitous veil of trepidation in this part of the country. We keep people honest."

"Who do I know who interests you?" Vern asked.

"That is not important at the moment," said Stone. "I'm not afraid to use your invention," he added. "I am intrigued by it."

Vern looked relieved.

"You need to be patient," Stone remarked. "Others have wrongly accused 'cloners' in the past based on what they thought were reliable facts. They were surprised to find that their 'facts' were carefully constructed bait that unwittingly, and successfully, lured a private society like ours to reveal itself and be destroyed. If some group has managed to clone humans in secrecy you should expect that they will be protected in ways that you have not yet imagined."

Vern thought for a moment. "So if I am right and one of these communities is a colony of clones I probably can't count on you for much support."

"That depends," Stone answered. "Don't lose sight of the fact that machines with human characteristics have been around for more than a decade now. The newer ones are only built for special purposes. They are engineered so that they don't become physically and intellectually stronger than people. They are universally distrusted, which is why they are monitored through mandatory digital tracking systems, so they don't become a threat. Real human clones living anonymously within a regular community of humans would be a breakthrough. If you are planning on barging into one of these communities on your own, then we never knew each other. If you have a different idea, I am ready to listen."

"I tested my own photograph in the software," Vern told Stone. "I don't have a twin, yet the software found a positive result. Someone who looks and sounds exactly like me."

It was a far less conclusive result than the ones that Vern had observed previously for other test cases. His double appeared to stay in different locations every few days, using multiple aliases. The double did not have a regular address. It had gone for weeks on end with no Internet or smartphone communication that could be easily traced.

"I see," Stone remarked. "Your interest in hunting clones is personal."

"I feel threatened," said Vern.

"I believe that the prospect of our identity being shared by an exact duplicate would frighten most people," said Stone. "It is a visceral fear of the unknown that breeds perpetual insecurity. What if your double is stronger? Smarter? What if it is psychotic and you are held responsible for its actions? Individual identity was not meant to be shared."

"I am having difficulty accepting that I have a double," said Vern. "Perpetual insecurity. That's what drives you to fight cloning?"

"Not entirely," Stone answered. "Creating artificial life is against the will of God. He is the creator. Not humans."

Vern's computer began sounding an alarm.

"What does that mean?" Stone asked.

"It says that my double has resurfaced." The signal only lasted a few seconds, but it was enough to get a lock. "He is nearby."

Stone grew more attentive. "This is your moment to make history, so long as you are certain about your method. Find him. We must test him to be sure that he has your DNA. He is like you. Same strengths. Same weaknesses. Who better than you to know how to create the circumstances for him to meet with one of us. Text this number when you are ready. I'll make sure that the right people are in place."

Stone stood up and excused himself, leaving Vern to ponder how to confront his double.

CHAPTER 3

Water cascaded down the fountain in the middle of River Park behind the bench where the Inspector sat expectantly.

"You're late," the Inspector said to the man who sat down beside him.

"You look nervous," Devon Granger remarked.

"No I don't," replied the Inspector. "I look concerned. I've seen the reports. Small groups of opportunistic young men outsmarting terrorists. I don't buy it."

"Your chief buys it," Devon said. "If you are no longer interested my group can leave. You will likely have to explain why an attack that could have been prevented was allowed to take place."

The Inspector thought for a moment.

"You have authorization for half the payment, don't you?"

"I'm not used to paying this kind of bounty," the Inspector said. He pulled out his mobile phone and transferred half of the funds to an account number that Devon gave him. "These bombings and shootings are becoming too common," he added in frustration. "Tell me your plan."

"Our main man will be sitting at that table closest to the street," Devon explained as he pointed to an outdoor cafe. "They are going to send two of their men to meet him. We'll have a couple of spotters in contact via mobile phones filming the whole exercise from the apartments on either side of the courtyard. Drones are too risky, they'll blow our cover. One of our men will be in a boat in the river, right behind where our main guy will spring the trap. Just in case things don't go according to plan. Once they hand over the money, our main guy and the two targets will walk over to the street. Your team will pick the three of them up in the van and take them to where the suspects think the weapons and explosives are. Our man will walk away when you collar the perpetrators. You will have saved the day."

"It's too easy," said the Inspector.

"This is supposed to be the easy part," Devon replied. "We've done the hard work already. Meeting them. Gaining their trust. Convincing them that we can get them the destructive power they require."

The Inspector remained skeptical.

"Our story is simple," Devon added. "We act as if we are as radicalized as they are. We explain how we have the inside track to get the hardware needed for their cause. Law enforcement has clamped down so hard on the freedoms of people and movement of goods in these Red Zones. We present ourselves as a supplier most radicals will believe in. We get the explosives, the detonators, the special ammunition. We take all the risk. We look like we fit into the general population. Why wouldn't they take the bait?"

The Inspector gave Devon a stare of displeasure.

"Don't forget we called you when we figured out the plot. If your people had been tuned in my team wouldn't be here to get paid."

"Where is the rest?" the Inspector asked.

"Phone numbers, call transcripts, safe house addresses, credit card numbers, bank accounts they're all here," Devon said as he showed the Inspector a memory card. "You get these later today, once you have the punks locked up and I get the rest of the money."

Two hours later Devon emerged from one of the apartments. He went back to the park bench by the fountain. He sat down, placed a small receiver in one of his ears then checked in with each member of the team. The Inspector's van had just rolled into position down the street to his right. Devon gave the word. A few moments later Kalan Mars emerged and took a seat at a table that overlooked the river.

A few stragglers extended their stay on the restaurant patio to enjoy the sunshine a little longer. Some patrons had come for a late lunch, to miss the crowds. Two men strolled casually in front of the patio, in a manner that tried to conceal that they were searching for something. One of them stopped when he saw the open vintage cigarette pack. That was the clue. The pair were convinced enough to stand by the table.

"I thought you were trying to quit. Smoking is bad for your health," one of the men said.

"I don't smoke. These are for you," Kalan replied. "Go ahead. Take one," he added, pulling a lighter from one of his pockets. The coded message was complete.

The two men sat down at the table. One nervously looked around. The other spoke to Kalan.

"We need to go. Where is the vehicle?"

"Don't be in such a rush. Have a smoke."

One of the men reached for a smoke. The other expressed concern. "We got no time."

"Show me the money. Then we can be on our way," said Kalan. The Inspector's van started to move slowly toward them.

One of the men pulled his phone out to make the electronic transfer. Kalan punched in the password, then watched the transaction finish. The man reached for his phone. It fell to the ground. Kalan leaned to one side and reached over to pick it up. Something whizzed past Kalan's ear.

A gaping hole opened suddenly in the chest of the man across the table. He writhed backward, before lurching forward and crashing onto the table. Blood gushed everywhere. He fell from his chair then convulsed rapidly on the ground.

The lone suspect lept to his feet. He looked around frantically for a place to run. Undercover officers piled out of the van and bolted toward him. Kalan crouched down. He looked back to where he thought the bullet must have been fired from. A man walked away slowly on the other side of the road, far behind where the Inspector's van was parked.

Devon retreated quickly and ducked down behind the fountain. "What's going on?" he asked the spotters in a panicked voice.

"I don't know," came one reply. "Looks like the cops fired a shot. It came from the direction of their van," said the other.

Devon had to raise his voice so that he would be heard over the screaming and commotion. "Where's Kalan?"

"Long gone by now," replied the spotter. "He made it to the boat. We're out of here. Cops are heading your way, Devon. You don't have much time."

Devon and the spotters disappeared down different side streets in the small city of Birchstone while the chaos ensued. They made their separate ways to an old warehouse on the outskirts of town later that evening.

"Anyone heard from Kalan or the boatman?" one of the spotters asked. Blank stares gave him the answer.

"What do we do now?" asked the other spotter.

"Let's figure that out after we understand what happened today," Devon remarked quietly.

One of the spotters furnished a small, thin computer. "I shot some wide-angle video of the whole area for about ten minutes leading up to when Kalan arrived." Devon and the other spotter devoted all of their attention to the screen. "Look down the road a few seconds after the police van pulls into position." The video ran in slow motion.

"Looks like some guy crossed the road," the other spotter noted.

"Now look at it magnified."

"Some guy carrying a long case walks towards a hedge wall and then doesn't come out the other side," Devon remarked.

"Here is a short clip right after the shooting."

"The man is walking away from the hedge wall wearing a different jacket, the same pants carrying a backpack. It's blurred," the other spotter remarked. "Can't quite make out his face."

"Yeah, I was a little shaken at that point," said the first spotter. "Couldn't hold the camera straight. Check out this still image. It's a side by side comparison of the mystery man at five times magnification. Before and after the shooting."

Devon gazed at the image in disbelief. "It's grainy, but that guy looks just like Kalan."

"That's what I thought," the first spotter added.

"So the cops planted a sniper," said the second spotter. "They had their own plan to take down the suspects. It was less expensive than working with us."

"Sure, that's one way of looking at it," the first spotter replied. "This clip might change your mind." A short, slow-motion clip showed Kalan moving to the side just in time for the man in front of him take the bullet. The close-up images were at full magnification. "If the guy in the hedge wall took that shot, he wasn't aiming for our customer," said the first spotter. "He was aiming for Kalan."

"That raises more questions than it answers," Devon remarked.

"Our cover is blown," said the first spotter.

"As for what we do now, my vote is that we split up and go our separate ways," the second spotter added. "At least until this episode fades into memory."

The first spotter concurred.

"Give me my share of today's proceeds and I'll be gone," said the second spotter.

"You want to quit?" Devon asked.

"Yeah, I do," the second spotter replied.

"Forget it," Devon replied. "I'm going to get the rest of what we are owed from the Inspector. Then you'll get your share."

"What?"

"I need to get to the cops before they do something stupid, like post my picture with a request for the general public to be on the lookout for me. We didn't do anything wrong. I'm going to set the Inspector straight."

"Here you go," one of the spotters said as he gave Devon the small computer. "You might need this."

"Thanks," Devon replied. "Before we all disappear into the night, I need you two to watch over me for one last encounter." He called the Inspector and arranged the meeting.

XXXX

"Who's your comrade?" Devon asked when he approached the Inspector at the bar in the Six Flags Hotel.

"Deputy Chief Wilson," he replied.

"Looks like your star is rising Inspector," Devon remarked. "Foiling a terror attack in this part of the country. Congratulations. Where's the rest of our money?"

"Who is your man?" the Inspector asked.

"The man who you guys almost shot?" Devon inquired.

"It wasn't us," the Inspector retorted.

"You don't need to know," Devon replied.

"Look, son," said the Deputy Chief calmly. "We'll get your cooperation one way or the other."

"Not unless you pay up," Devon replied defiantly.

The Inspector pulled out his mobile phone and grudgingly satisfied Devon's request.

"That's much better. Here you go," Devon responded as he handed the Inspector the memory card. "All of the information you need is there. Phone numbers, call transcripts, safe house addresses, credit card numbers, bank accounts, as promised."

The Inspector fumbled with the memory card for a moment.

"Don't be spreading stories about the shooting in the press. Blowing my cover will come back to haunt you," Devon added.

The Deputy Chief frowned.

"Have you figured out why Birchstone made it onto a list of terrorist targets?" Devon asked.

"The suspect who lived has not been as helpful as we had hoped," the Inspector replied.

"Data centers," Devon proposed. "Camouflaged by the well-publicized out-migration of youth that hides the gradual arrival and concentration of information technology experts. Birchstone is a perfect cover to locate strategic assets. Close to bigger cities, but quiet enough not to draw mainstream attention. If those assets were destroyed, telecommunications within our borders and amongst our military around the world would be disrupted. It's all on the card I just gave you."

"I could get sacked for this escapade," the Inspector complained.

"Who gets sacked when a terrorist attack is foiled with no collateral damage, especially when a hoard of new intelligence is discovered?" Devon asked rhetorically. "It would have been different if our man had taken that bullet. Your sniper is the one who should be sacked."

"No one on our force fired that bullet," the Deputy Chief responded forcefully.

"A picture trumps a thousand lies," said Devon as he showed the officers an image on the tablet computer. The Deputy Chief looked dismayed. The shot came from the direction of the van. "You have surveillance equipment everywhere in this city. My guess is that you have seen this already," Devon added.

The Deputy Chief looked over at the Inspector, then Devon. "Mister Granger, the shooter wasn't one of ours. We'll see to it that the local press won't find out anything about your group. We'll find a way to make this story disappear quickly. You are free to go. We have no further questions. The Chief asked me to pass along his gratitude to you and your associates for bringing knowledge of this impending attack to our attention. Harnessing young men for a good cause is rare. Good night."

Devon stayed behind. The spotters left their vantage points on the hotel mezzanine and joined him after the police officers left.

"It has been a good run," said Devon. "We've made great coin by helping cops foil terror plans all across these Red Zones. I don't know how we can keep going without Kalan."

"Anyone heard from him?" the second spotter asked.

"He's pretty spooked is my guess," Devon replied. "Kalan is long gone. Who knows when we will hear from him again."

CHAPTER 4

"You don't belong with these other men," the young woman remarked.

Kalan looked up. He hadn't noticed her. He chose to eat his dinner alone in the shelter, far away from the others in the cafeteria. Sounds of men yelling in the alley across the street had distracted him.

"May I join you?" she asked.

Kalan pointed to the chair across from him. "What makes you say that?" he asked after she sat down.

"All of these men are homeless. Most of them are addicts. A few of them are even crazy. You don't look to be affected by any of those conditions."

"You work here?" Kalan asked.

"Afternoons and evenings," she replied. "You look like a man on the run."

"Worked here long?" Kalan asked.

"Long enough to recognize someone who needs a place to hide."

"It's that obvious?"

"Yes, it is. That's why I came over to speak with you. Most people who need to hide with us try to blend in more with that crowd," she said pointing to the other side of the room. "People on the run who show up here are often violent criminals. You stand out. Someone will call the authorities to check you out sooner than later. I can help you."

"I don't think so," Kalan replied.

"You must have a name."

"Kalan."

"What are you running from Kalan?"

"You wouldn't believe me if I told you."

"I've heard many stories from guys like you. Tell me your tale. Then I'll tell you if I believe you."

"I was sitting at a table outside on a patio. I turned around and saw someone who looked exactly like me off in the distance. Just after he tried to shoot me."

"That doesn't tell me why you came to our shelter."

"I didn't get your name," Kalan remarked with a distracted look.

"Rain," the woman answered.

"A Haven City, like this one, is big enough for me to disappear into the woodwork. No one will think to look for me here."

"At least not yet," Rain replied. She paused to think for a moment. "I figure you must have grown up somewhere around here. You chose to come home. You're gambling that you know this city better than an adversary who is looking for you."

"If that's what you think what should I do now?" Kalan asked.

"You're not giving me much to go on," said Rain. "I don't know why you can't go home or go to friends to lay low. I can't help you if you don't tell me what you need. You are starting to sound a little bit crazy, like some of these other people."

"That guy can probably track me down anywhere. For all I know he's figured out who my friends and family are and he's scouting out where they live right now. Hoping that I'll show up for help. Besides, I don't know if I can trust any of them. I was with a few of my friends when that bullet whizzed by my head."

"You must know this person. He must be a twin or a cousin, something like that," said Rain.

"I don't have a twin or a cousin that looks like me."

Rain thought about what Kalan had said. "Sounds like you are running for your life."

"You are as smart as you are attractive, Rain," Kalan replied. "I need to settle in for the night. I'll be up early tomorrow."

Kalan stood up to take his dinner tray back to the counter. Noise from across the street grew more intense. Bottles breaking were soon surpassed by the sound of gunfire. He settled back into his chair. Sirens whirred off in the distance.

"This place always gets searched when there is trouble nearby," said Rain. "You can come with me if you want."

"To go where?" Kalan asked.

"Somewhere safe, at least for tonight."

"Safe. Really? How do I know that?"

"You don't," said Rain. "Trust me, or stay here. You decide."

XXXX

"I thought you would have been here sooner," Kalan said as Rain slipped through the door into the small hallway of the abandoned distillery.

"How did you get in here? I told you to wait outside."

"I don't have the luxury of waiting outside. Even if it is dark. Even if I'm in a place as out of the way as this."

"At least you had the sense not to try and get through this door," Rain said as took out her keys.

"What kind of creature lurks behind your door?" Kalan asked.

"You left the shelter just in time. It was searched from top to bottom. That's why I'm late."

Kalan cautiously followed Rain into her space under the watchful glare of her large, muscular boxer. She took hold of the mighty dog's collar and locked him in the small hallway that separated her space from the one next door.

Kalan walked into the center of the room. Unfinished paintings sat on a small collection of easels. Images depicting torment, in a style Kalan had never seen before, hung from the walls. "Did I paint them? Is that what you are wondering?"

"They are bold," Kalan remarked. "Nothing like flowers or landscapes or..."

"What did you expect?" Rain asked. "Rainbows and sunsets? These works are how I see our times. People dying with diseases that antibiotics used to fight. Irregular supplies of food and water. Air that is almost too thick with smog to breathe some days. Migration inland away from the rising ocean. Add those up and you get desperation. Poverty. Sickness."

Kalan wandered further into the room. "I would never have expected the inside of this building to be so remarkable judging by its appearance on the outside," he said while looking around.

Off to one side stood a large, unfinished sculpture that extended from the floor almost to the ceiling. A man's figure was emerging from the wood and rock.

"What's this going to be when it is done?" Kalan asked.

"I haven't decided," said Rain. "Maybe he will overcome the hardships of our world and breakthrough to something better. Maybe he will personify the fear in our world."

"Do you work with a gallery?" Kalan asked.

"If I finished him in the image of fear in our society you might have something in common with him."

"Me?" Kalan remarked.

"There was a shooting in Red Zone Nine yesterday afternoon. Like the one you described at the shelter. Some terrorist got shot and died later in hospital. The bullet just missed a young man sitting near him. I figure you're that young man."

"Where did you hear that?"

"That's not important. Back at the shelter, you said that I wouldn't believe your story. I am starting to believe. That's why I showed up."

"Maybe I should move on. Stay somewhere else tonight."

"Suit yourself," Rain replied. "You will be safe here. Nobody else knows where you are."

"Did you see a picture of the shooter?" Kalan asked.

"No," said Rain. "The best thing for you right now is to unwind, get some rest."

"You're sure no one else knows I'm here."

"Yes, I'm sure. One other person knows that I have a guest tonight. He doesn't know who you are. He also knows that I only bring strange men home for the night when they need help."

"Who is he?" Kalan asked.

"Cecil will stop by in a few minutes. He calls himself the Superintendent. He'll show you to your room."

"Where is it?"

"Just through there," Rain said, pointing to a door Kalan had not noticed before.

"What would you do tomorrow morning if you were me?" Kalan asked.

"We're going to meet with a friend of mine. A doctor who can access the DNA records from all of the births going back well over thirty years. She works in a clinic that handles pathology and forensics. Cold cases. Wrongful convictions. Crimes that can only be solved by high-powered science. She has the tools to get around the barriers that the establishment puts up in order to keep secrets. You can ask her questions about your biological parents and siblings. Perhaps she can help."

There was a knock at the door. "That will be Cecil. The answer to your question is yes. I do work with galleries. My inspiration comes from how people in distress, like you, survive. Sleep well."

XXXX

"You look surprised Mister Mars," said the Doctor.

"I had no idea that..."

"Newborns are always screened for genetic diseases," she remarked. "Government-mandated. Parental consent is not required. Hasn't been for a while. Your DNA is in the records somewhere."

"Really?"

"I just need a sample," the Doctor added as she handed Kalan a swab.

"What do we do now?" Kalan asked.

"Take a seat," she replied, as she pointed to a waiting room. "We will have some preliminary results for you within the hour."

Kalan walked over to the waiting room, while Rain had a quiet conversation with her friend. The room was bright and full of people who sought relief from some form of ailment. Security cameras were mounted in every corner. He became anxious.

"You should know more soon enough," Rain said once she joined Kalan. "I need to go now."

"I can't stay here," Kalan remarked. "These people, the cameras," he added nervously. "We walked past a church on the way here. Let's go there. It will be dark inside. No people. No cameras."

"I really need to get on with the rest of my day," Rain insisted. "You're going to have to make some decisions about where to go next. I can't help you make them. Besides, if you need anything you know where the shelter is."

Kalan followed Rain as she walked out of the clinic. "It's right there," he said, looking over at the church. Rain changed her mind, for the meantime.

"Do you have a number they can text you at when your results are ready?" Rain asked once they were inside the chapel.

"No," Kalan replied. "Better that no one knows how to track me down."

Rain resisted the urge to leave. "I get it. She has my number."

"Who has your number?"

"Mia, the doctor you met with."

Kalan felt safe, at least for the moment. He and Rain sat cloaked in the darkness that shrouded the rear pew of the empty church. Candles flickered along the sides. The lone cleric tended to the ones on the other side. Sunlight brought the colors in the windows near the altar to life.

"Thank you for helping me," Kalan said quietly.

Rain simply nodded.

"What makes you so interested in the desperate souls of this world?" he asked, as the two sat on the wooden bench, looking toward the altar.

"Desperate souls fight to survive. They live on the raw edge between life and death. That inspires me. Seems like I was born to see the world this way."

Rain looked down as the cleric walked slowly by them. He turned and came back. He was an older man. He looked over at Kalan.

"I know you," he remarked.

"You must be mistaken," Kalan answered. "I have never been here before."

The old man persisted. "I am not mistaken. You were in my congregation down south. You're Zach Gedder's boy. I'm sure of it."

Rain tried to get Kalan's attention.

"I remember when you started coming to fellowship with your father and sister," the cleric remarked. "Must be fifteen years ago now."

Kalan wanted to ask the clergyman some questions, but Rain intervened. "We need to go," she said. "Now."

XXXX

"This room is private," the Doctor assured Kalan and Rain. "We can speak freely.

"What did you find out?" Kalan asked.

"I can get information that most people can't access," Mia remarked. "But you can't know that. Do you understand?"

"This discussion that we are about to have never happened is what you are saying," Kalan confirmed.

"No. You just can't tell anyone that I am your source of information." Mia replied. "Medical records turned up the same DNA in two places," Mia noted. "Once in what is now Haven City Four and once in a suburb of Red Zone Nine. Where did you grow up?"

"Hadley's Crossing."

"Where on Earth is that?"

"Here," Kalan replied, showing her a map on his mobile phone.

"I see," said Mia. "I found that the first birth record was normal. The second birth record appears to have been tampered with, perhaps even falsified. The birth dates are eleven months apart. This is where I think the records were manipulated. The second birth was signed off by Damien Farlane."

"Who?"

"Doctor Damien Farlane pioneered several techniques that enabled the creation of synthetic lifeforms. He is a recluse today if he is even still alive. At the time the baby was born, he was suspected of cloning humans, even though it was, and still is, against the law. Rumors have persisted for a long time about Farlane's ability to clone humans. No one has ever found any proof. I don't believe that you have a twin Mister Mars, but there is someone else who is exactly like you."

"That's quite a story," Kalan remarked. "You expect me to believe this?"

"I understand this must be a shock for you," Mia remarked. "You came here this morning confident of your identity and now you are told that you might be someone else."

"You think that I was adopted, or cloned?"

"Can't rule it out," Mia answered.

"How can I be sure?"

"If my theory is correct there are no records of adoption. If you believe the urban myths, Farlane had a network of families who could not have children of their own. He provided them with clones. It was faster than trying to adopt. Birth certificates were forged. The families went on with their lives. If you want to be sure you need to find Doctor Farlane."

"Who is a recluse whose whereabouts are unknown," Kalan added.

"Precisely," Mia added. "He is probably as interested in finding you as you are in finding him. If he is still alive."

"Why would he be?" Kalan asked.

"If Doctor Farlane successfully created a community of clones over the past few decades he would want to know if any of them suffered the poor health and immune system failures that plagued early experiments with cloning animals. My guess is that he wants to keep an eye on all of his creations. Your parents must be part of the network. Ask them how to reach Doctor Farlane."

"Can you tell if I am the original, or if I am the clone?" Kalan asked.

"I have no way of knowing," Mia answered. "Doctor Farlane will know the answer."

Kalan looked over at Rain.

37

"Let's go someplace and talk," Rain said.

"Please wait outside in the hall Mister Mars," Mia added. "I need to speak with Rain for a moment."

Kalan walked out, confused.

"Stories about Damien Farlane have been floating around for years," Mia remarked quietly. "I dismissed them all as groundless speculation until I saw those two birth records and identical DNA samples. I have dealt with many identity cases, but I have never seen one like this before."

"Do you know anything about Farlane?"

"No, not really," Mia replied. "If you believe the urban mythology powerful people want to bring Farlane to justice. Other powerful people want access to his secrets. My guess is that you will become a very rich woman if you can make either of those happen. Or, you will end up dead. Think about how are you going to play this situation. You likely don't have much time."

"Are you in any danger?" Rain asked Mia.

"No, I'll be fine. I hacked this information with secure aliases."

"Thanks for helping me out. I owe you one," Rain said as she left the office.

Kalan and Rain walked for a few minutes to a small park before he felt like talking.

"We hear about robots that behave like people. Machine intelligence that will surpass human intelligence. Experiments with editing genes. Farming organs. It all seems to take place on the periphery of our lives. There is a buzz about it for a while then it goes away. You just don't care that much because it doesn't affect you. Then someone who knows more about science than you do looks you in the eye and says that someone else might be you."

"Try to relax," said Rain.

"I'm furious," Kalan blurted out. "Have I been lied to my whole life? You saw that guy in the church earlier, saying that he recognized me. I am an only child. I don't have a sister. I've never been to church in my life. I don't know who I am anymore."

Rain reached out and took Kalan's hand. "Go back to my place. Lay low. In case you are being watched, get to this address first. I'll make sure that Cecil knows to expect you. There is an old tunnel. It leads to the distillery underground. He'll see to it that you get to my place in one piece."

Kalan thought about Rain's offer. Perhaps a safe place to rest was what he needed. Maybe she knew too much. Perhaps a safe place would tie him down. Perhaps he should keep moving. Her intentions seemed genuine. "Fine," he replied.

A few minutes after Rain left to go to the shelter Kalan strolled out from beneath the tree cover in the park and unsuspectingly into full view of surveillance cameras on the rooftops of nearby buildings. He worked up the nerve to make the call. He nervously dialed the number.

Jane Mars didn't recognize the number when her phone rang. On any other morning, she would be out in the yard tending to her garden. "Mother," he said.

"Kalan," she said in a surprised tone. "You sound exhausted."

"Is Dad there?"

Jane shook her head. "No. He's away until tomorrow."

"Might make things easier," Kalan said.

"You can't shoot your mouth off like the last time and expect to come back here whenever you want. You're a grown man. You need to act like it."

"I'm not calling to try and fix the past. I don't need a scolding. I need to find Damien Farlane."

There was a long silence.

"I don't have much time," Kalan said. "I need to know. Some guy who looks exactly like me tried to kill me. Then someone told that me I have a sister. What is going on?"

"We need to have this conversation in person. We can't speak about this over the phone."

"That's not going to happen any time soon," Kalan replied. "I need to stay hidden. How can I reach this Farlane guy?"

"I can't tell you that. Where are you Kalan?"

"That is nobody's business."

"Doctor Farlane doesn't take appointments on request," Jane remarked. "If he wants to see you he will find you."

"So it's true," Kalan remarked.

"I don't know what you have been told Kalan," Jane answered. "Come home for a while."

Kalan hung up.

XXXX

Cecil was a bigger man in the late afternoon light than Kalan remembered from the night before. "Rain told me to keep an eye on you. She thinks that you're pretty wound up." Kalan was silent.

The two disappeared into the underground tunnel.

"I don't want any trouble. I just want to get some rest," Kalan said as the pair emerged from the tunnel into the hallway that led to Rain's space in the old distillery.

"The room is all yours," Cecil said. "What are you running from? If you don't mind me asking."

"I wish I knew," Kalan replied.

"You go on and rest up," Cecil encouraged.

XXXX

A few hours later Rain shook him with vigor.

"What's going on?" Kalan asked slowly, as he opened his eyes to find Rain leaning over him.

"Sit up," Rain said in an agitated tone. "What do you make of this?" she asked. She handed Kalan a photograph.

Kalan took a few moments to collect his thoughts. "Where did you get this? Looks like it was taken this afternoon in the park when I called my mother."

"An older woman brought it around to the shelter, asking if anyone recognized you. One of the guys on the kitchen staff asked her what she wanted. He played it right. Didn't say that we had seen you. Didn't say that we hadn't."

"What did she want?" Kalan asked.

"She said that the person in this photograph is looking for someone." Rain handed Kalan a note. "This is where you need to be tomorrow at one o'clock. You need to go alone."

"If they knew how to get this note to you at the shelter, they must have followed you here," Kalan remarked.

"Nobody followed me here. I took the same tunnel you did. No witnesses. No cameras."

"They must know that I'm here."

"That's impossible," Rain replied calmly.

"What if it isn't?" Kalan protested. "The people who want me dead took that picture of me a few hours ago. At the park. Just after you left. They knew how to get it to you. So that you would pass it on to me. They must know that I am here."

Rain walked over to pet her boxer. "If he is right will you keep us safe?" she asked her dog, playfully. Rain looked back towards Kalan. "Maybe the people who want you dead are connected to this photograph. Maybe they aren't. Do they want to get to Farlane? Do they

41

work for Farlane? No point fretting over it tonight. You will know soon enough."

CHAPTER 5

People walked past Kalan as if he were invisible. He stood recessed in the shadows beside The Harrington Hotel, between 18th Street and 19th Street. Ozone fouled the dank humid city air. It left an aftertaste worse than the smoke from the pervasive forest fires that burned beyond the suburbs, in the Red Zone south of the Blue Zone border. He peered keenly through the haze down the street into the main square, wondering why there were two people fitting the description of the one person he had come to meet. Two men, each wearing long light-colored trench coats and dark glasses, had staked out space in opposite corners. Kalan watched how they grew restless once the meeting time had come and gone. The tension between them reached the breaking point.

When the man furthest away made the first move, Kalan decided it was time to leave. He walked away briskly, in the opposite direction. He heard the commotion but did not stop to watch. A big man of color caught up to Kalan and said "Go in here," as he ushered him into the old museum. "You don't have much time."

Moments later, Kalan found himself alone with the bulky stranger in one of the washrooms. The lock clicked shut.

"Who are you?" Kalan demanded, poised for a fight.

"That was smart," the man replied as he took off his coat. "You did what I would have done. Left the scene just before it got out of hand. Put this on," he said as he unzipped a second coat from inside the one he was wearing and tossed it to Kalan. "Quickly."

Kalan was reluctant, not ready to let his defenses down. However, the man across from him wasn't hankering for a fight. He pulled off his tearaway pants, revealing the shapely legs of a woman, from below a short leather skirt. A tattoo of a miniature Samurai sword adorned one of her inner thighs, just above where a real sword was stored conveniently in a knee-high boot. She reached behind her head and yanked off the mask of a tough-looking black man, revealing a young woman with long dark hair and deep brown eyes. Her speech was softer than Kalan would have imagined, once she peeled the thin audio distortion film away from her neck. "Put this on too," she said, handing Kalan a different latex mask.

"Tell me Dagger Lady, who is Farlane?" Kalan demanded.

The woman spoke quietly when she made the phone call. "We need to get out of here," she said to Kalan, ignoring his request. "Head for the silver car with the red wheels. I told it to wait for us."

Kalan, disguised as an older Latino man, walked casually with Dagger Lady down 19th Street. The man from the main square passed them as he rushed to zone in for the kill, oblivious that his prey was camouflaged, strolling away in the opposite direction. He was not the man who had been sent to protect Kalan. That man was dead. Dagger Lady remained composed but wary. She reached down into her boot to retrieve her weapon. It would be an easy kill if required.

Trench Coat took note of the silver car, thinking that it would make for a perfect getaway. He walked away in search of Kalan. Dagger Lady stood down.

XXXX

"Entering Danor Township," the computer remarked. Neither of them had spoken a word in the hour since leaving the old museum and traveling northeast of the

44

city. When the car came to rest beside a secluded house, Dagger Lady broke the silence. "You will be safe here."

Kalan took his mask off and wandered around to the back of the house. "I don't think your definition of safe is the same as mine," he remarked. He peered through the screen door. A gentle tug on the handle was enough for the slightly bent metal door frame to creak open. "Unlocked. You don't seem to be the trusting type." He walked inside, ready to take on any nemesis that was waiting for him. "You live here?"

"I stay here occasionally." Dagger Lady replied. "If required."

Kalan walked through the spartan bungalow. The curtains were slightly yellowed. The couch was almost worn through in places. Rust stained the porcelain sink and tub in the small bathroom. Barely exposed shiny round handles tucked into tiny spaces throughout the house caught his eye.

"There's not much in here," Kalan noted. "Except for this computer screen here on the table."

"You might want to thank me," Dagger Lady remarked.

"For what? Bringing me to a secluded place where you can kill me without anyone knowing. You could slit my throat with that sword in your boot, bury my remains out there in the wilderness and keep it a secret forever," Kalan said pointing to the vast open space behind the house. "At least the air is better here."

"For saving your life."

"I could have taken that guy on my own. You intervened for your own reasons. Where is Farlane?"

"This situation is much bigger than you," said a voice from the computer. The visual image of a bald, elderly man with a look of stern intensity came to life. "Sit down. I'm going to tell you some of what you need to know."

"Damien Farlane," said Kalan.

"If that's what you want to believe," the man replied.

Kalan reached down his shirt behind his shoulder. He pulled out his Silent Destroyer laser pistol, put in on the table and began to drum the fingers of one hand lightly on the barrel. "I don't care for the drama," he remarked dryly. "Just tell me what is going on."

"You're a man on the run, you're not a killer," the voice said. "Nisha is not going to hurt you."

Kalan clasped the weapon. Once the sensor confirmed his fingerprint the power meter pulsed to maximum.

"Stand up," Kalan said calmly.

Nisha nervously did as she was told.

"Turn around, then put one hand back on the table," said Kalan. "Take your boots off with your other hand. Slowly. Who knows where you may have blades stashed away. I want them all. Keep facing the other way, reach behind and put them on the table. That hand comes off the table and you'll get fried." he added. "I'm not in a trusting mood right now."

Nisha awkwardly did what she was told. Kalan collected a pair of Kunai swords, before switching off his pistol and placing it back on the table in front of him.

"So Farlane, where do we go from here?"

"This display of antisocial violent paranoia is disturbing," said the bald man on the screen. "You have become a mystery Kalan Mars. You were such a pleasant boy when you were young. Then you left home. You're just not the young man I expected."

"Am I a clone?"

"I prefer not to talk about who is on the list and who is not on the list when others are in the room. I only discuss the list with people face to face. Nisha is one of my assistants. She has never seen the list."

"Answer the question."

"I don't know what you were told. All I can say is that you grew up in the tranquil setting that I helped create for you."

"Hadley's Crossing is a colony, isn't it? A place where humans who were grown in test tubes live without knowing their true identity."

"Who told you this?"

"No one," Kalan replied. "It's my hunch."

"People who couldn't have children and who found the process of adoption too long and onerous came to me because I provided another option. They agreed to keep a secret in exchange for the fulfillment of their wishes."

"The secret of who is a freak and who isn't?"

"Now you sound like them, Kalan."

"Them?"

"Self-proclaimed protectors of human biology. The Society for the Elimination of Artificial People. The Church of Pure Humanity. The most dangerous adversaries you have at the moment."

Kalan listened intently.

"They convinced politicians to initiate Fear of Clone legislation. All that has to happen for those laws to be enacted is proof that a clone exists at large in society. That's the world we will soon live in Kalan. Two human beings will have exactly the same DNA. One will be free. The other will be reviled, labeled as an unworthy replica. Destined to be an outcast and openly discriminated against."

"Who was the man in the park today?"

"One of them," the bald man on the screen replied. "A zealot who thinks you are a replica." The bald man's face grew dour. "He found a way to break through the defenses that protect your secret. Others will follow. They won't rest until they have captured you. Perhaps not even until you are dead."

"Who are these people?"

47

"Nisha can tell you about them later. We have a more pressing matter to deal with. Someone told you about Farlane," the man on the screen persisted. "Who was it?"

"That's not important."

"It is very important. You are the only one in the colony who has any awareness of the situation. As far as I can tell."

"What does that have to do with anything?" said Kalan defiantly.

"You are the only one who has any reason to suspect that their identity is different from what they were raised to believe. Keeping that secret is worth something. If the secret gets out, lives will be destroyed."

"I wouldn't know anything about that," Kalan said.

"I took every precaution for this not to happen. You must believe me. My enemies are closer to finding the secret than I thought, based on what I have learned since yesterday. You called your mother."

"That is how we found out that you know something of Doctor Farlane," Nisha added. "One of these cults must know how to track your whereabouts. They likely know the whereabouts of your double. Two people with the same DNA who resemble each other as twins would go a long way to proving their case that cloning has been practiced for some time. Won't matter to them if you're dead or alive."

"What would you do if you were me?" Kalan asked.

"You must find your double," the man said firmly. "Find him before he finds you. Then bring him to me."

Frustration was written on Kalan's face. "How am I supposed to do that and why should I trust you?"

"Nisha will guide you," the bald man replied. "You must trust her."

"I'll take a pass on that," said Kalan. "You want to keep me in this dingy house just as long as it suits you."

"I'm not sure that you have many choices," the man concluded. The image on the screen disappeared.

"You're harder to handle that I thought," Nisha griped.

Kalan sat back in his chair. "One of Damien Farlane's assistants. Bet that's a plum job," he said.

Nisha took the young man's insolence in stride. "You don't need to know why I do this kind of work."

"So you're a doctor and a killer?" Kalan surmised. "Those skills don't usually go hand in hand. What's in this for you?"

"Doctor Farlane's work has created people with greater intellects, who are spared the most crippling diseases of our time. Cloning was just one step along the way. My place in that history is what's in it for me."

"I don't know a lot about modern science," Kalan replied. "I do know that I don't like being caught up in the unintended chaos. One day I'm living my life, the next day I'm a fugitive. Just because some people think that I was created in a lab. Bet it would be different if a clone were important. Someone famous."

"Doctor Farlane's work has always been managed carefully. If not, people die. This is about more than just you," Nisha said somberly. "Hatred. Fear of the unknown. They are as much at play here as are the virtues of scientific knowledge and the spirit of discovery," Nisha replied. "Some clones are already famous," she added confidently.

Kalan picked the Kunai swords up from the table and put them in his jacket. He stood up and walked slowly around the house once more. It became clear to him that the shiny round metal objects he observed earlier represented an arsenal of small swords. Dagger Lady was ready for battle. But with whom? He returned to the main room to look out of the windows, to see if anyone was visible in the distance. "How did you find me?"

Kalan asked nonchalantly, concealing that he had spotted the dagger handles.

"You called your mother and asked about Doctor Farlane. All of the colonists have word recognition software on their phones. If a keyword, like Farlane, or clone comes up in a conversation our network traces the position of the speakers through GPS. For safety reasons. We modified an old photograph of you to make it look as if you were at the park where you placed the call. One of our associates dropped off copies at places close to the park where we thought you might be staying."

Kalan thought about Nisha's answer. Something was wrong. The photo that Rain showed him looked too real to have been constructed from older images.

"Where were you staying?" Nisha asked.

Kalan ignored the question. "When I find my double how do I bring him to Farlane?"

"I'll tell you when you need to know," Nisha answered.

"How do I find this double?"

"He has the same strengths and weaknesses as you do," she answered. "Tell me how the strengths that you both share could be used against him and how the weaknesses that you both share could be used against you. Then I'll tell you how we can find him."

"I've seen my double," Kalan remarked. "Have you?"

Nisha was caught off guard, not sure what to say.

"That's what I thought," said Kalan. He reached for his weapon. "The only people who know about my double are trying to kill me. Do you know where he is right now?" The power meter registered maximum.

Nisha paused. "No," she sighed. "All I know is that he is coming for you."

Kalan's instincts told him that once the bald man signed off, he would dispatch whoever else Nisha would need to keep him under control. Nisha was his ticket to meet Doctor Farlane. He needed to act fast.

"Your plan is to keep me here until whoever is coming for me shows up."

"It's not what you think," Nisha said quietly.

"Empty your pockets here on the table," Kalan demanded.

"What's going on?" Nisha asked. "I just saved your..."

"You're setting me up," Kalan interrupted. He turned her mobile phone off and put it in his pocket. He motioned to the door. Nisha walked outside. "What do we do now?" she asked.

"Follow that path through the woods," Kalan insisted. "It leads to an old cemetery. There is a cabin that the caretaker used to live in. We're not that far from Hadley's Crossing. I used to come through here from time to time."

"Forget it," Nisha protested.

Kalan pulled her phone out. "I need a picture of the bald man," he remarked. "I need your number as well." He gave Nisha's phone back to her.

Nisha sent the picture and the number to Kalan's phone. Kalan stepped away briefly. The message he texted to Devon Granger was short. "Find this guy. Will check back soon." Kalan turned his phone back off.

"Tables are turned now. You need me more than I need you," Kalan told Nisha. "I can find Farlane on my own terms. You can stay here if you want to confront whoever is coming here to kill me. Come with me if you want to live another day."

"Why would I go with you? I'll be safer here," Nisha said calmly.

"You saved my life today. I owe you for that." The sounds of stones ricocheting off the metal panels of a vehicle that was closing in quickly could be heard in the distance. Whoever was coming for Kalan was closer than expected. Nisha looked worried. Kalan walked a few steps along the path before disappearing into the woods as the dark clouds rolled in. Nisha needed to make a choice: stay or follow Kalan.

CHAPTER 6

"You're back early," Jane Mars remarked as Don returned home from his trip. "Was it a good show?"

Don hugged his wife. "Seems like there's never a bad time to be selling weapons. The show ended early. Some big storm is blowing in from the south tonight. It's got people worked up. Most of us didn't want to stick around any longer than necessary," he said. He reached into the fridge and pulled out a beer. "You look out of sorts."

"I am out of sorts," Jane replied. "I don't want us to be the ones responsible for giving away Farlane's secret."

"Stop talking nonsense," Don replied calmly.

"It isn't nonsense, Don. What would the other families do? They would hate us," she said, answering her own question.

Don pulled the tab on his can of ale.

"Kalan called yesterday," she said.

"Did he say he was sorry?"

"He said that someone who looked just like him tried to kill him," Jane replied.

Don looked concerned. "Did he say how it happened?"

"He wasn't hurt," Jane replied. "Then he asked who Doctor Farlane was."

"Did you tell him?" Don asked.

"No. Of course I didn't tell him. I told him to come home so that we could talk," Jane retorted.

"What did he say?"

"He didn't say anything. He just hung up. I don't know what to think."

"Any idea who told him about Farlane?"

"No, but I've got a bad feeling this time," Jane said nervously.

Don paid more attention. "Did you try calling him back?"

"His phone has been off since he called. They're going to send someone aren't they?" Jane remarked.

"To do what?"

"Don't be so difficult," Jane insisted. "You remember when little Danny Brown was sick. The secret almost got out then. The spooks showed up and a day later the whole family moved away. Same thing with Debbie Young and then later with Barney Spikes. They're going to send someone to take us away. That's what the other families will want."

"I think you are overreacting. All the stuff you're talking about happened years ago."

"I am not overreacting," Jane rebuffed.

"What are you going to do?"

"We gotta leave Don. Right now."

"To go where?" he asked.

"I don't know," Jane replied, even more distressed.

"How about you call your sister," Don suggested. "Go stay with her for a few days. If you start packing now you could be there in a couple of hours. Before dark. Before the storm arrives."

Jane went upstairs to pack her things. Don stepped out into his backyard to relax. He sipped on his beer while admiring the forest on the west side of the property, just as one of the new Renegade Alien motorcycles blew past a remote traffic sensor on the south side of town.

XXXX

Vern Gedder left the scene before Stone found out that his shot had missed Kalan. Vern was on his own now, abandoned by leaders of the Society for the Elimination of Artificial People, but privately admired by some of the members. He wanted to control the element of surprise in taking the fight to his double. He figured that Kalan would have gone home as he raced his Renegade Alien towards Hadley's Crossing.

Flashing lights on the drone that flew beside him convinced Vern to slow down and stop at the side of the road. It only took a few moments for the police cruiser to pull up behind him. The officer walked slowly towards the biker as he motioned for Vern to open the cockpit and remove his helmet.

"Step away from the bike," the officer commanded. "Face away from the road and keep your hands visible."

Officer Drysdale walked slowly around the newest Renegade offering, with its deep red finish and metallic silver trim. The upgraded collapsible cockpit particularly caught his eye as the flexible acrylic was now much thinner and could now retract fully into the front forks just by pressing a touchpad key on the control panel. This new self-balancing design was more compact and sleek, even capable of autonomous control at low speed if the sensory inputs from the driver's eye and head movements were missing. The batteries were smaller, mostly to reduce weight, which capped the range at two hundred miles on a single charge. This machine was designed to redefine the experience of motorcycling. The officer was impressed.

"Stand up straight, spread your legs and hold your arms out to the sides," the officer requested as he shone a small beam outwards from a device on his belt.

"No firearms, that's a good sign. Show me your license," the officer requested. "Vern Gedder," the officer read out loud.

"That's right."

The southern accent gave him away. "My eyes must be fooling me. Could have sworn you were a local boy," the officer remarked.

Vern didn't know what to say.

"Those leathers look pretty tough," the officer noted. "Guess you need that kind of road rash protection on these new bikes," he added.

"The new metal reinforced leathers do the job," Vern replied.

"Folks from around here know that the speed limit drops back before that crest in the road. You rode over it doing almost three times the limit. You must have disabled your speed limiter." The officer took a moment to read the particulars on the license. "What brings you to Hadley's Crossing Mister Gedder?"

Vern turned to look back down the road. "Nothing in particular. Just passing through."

"Just passing through to where?" the officer asked.

"Riding east. Going to stop in all the big cities."

The officer scanned the license with the small mobile computer on his belt. "Your first ticket is for doing more than twice the speed limit." Then he scanned Vern's license again. "Your second ticket is for disabling the speed control on your bike."

"Can't you give me a break..."

"I could impound this fine machine and drive it away myself, except that you weren't doing three times the speed limit," the officer remarked. "Enjoy your stay in Hadley's Crossing," he added, looking confused as he walked slowly back to his car. He made a short call before driving away.

XXXX

"I'll call you when I get there," Jane said as she plucked her rain jacket from the closet beside the front door.

"Fine," Don replied. "Now go and relax."

"Who was on the phone a minute ago?" Jane called through the hall to the kitchen.

"Tom Drysdale," said Don.

"Officer Tom Drysdale? I was thinking about him the other day. Who could have imagined that such a teenage dork would turn into such a respectable member of our community? What did he want?"

"Nothing much. Said he came across someone who looked like someone I know. He was curious about the show. Wants to know how to get his hands on the next issue of Silent Destroyer's laser pistol before it goes on sale to the public."

Don watched from behind the sheer curtains in the front room until his wife drove around the corner leading further into the Blue Zone. He noticed the motorcycle parked up the road along the edge of the forest, by the top of the hill. He left the front screen door open and unlatched before walking back inside his house.

Night appeared to fall earlier than usual as the dark storm clouds moved in. Lightning flashed intermittently off to the south. Thunder rumbled loud enough to vibrate the windows in their panes. This was the address that Vern's software had tracked Kalan Mars to. Vern opened the front door slowly and let himself in.

Blackness filled the house. Flashes of lightning illuminated the interior. Vern flipped a switch beside the kitchen. Nothing happened. He took a step forward. The light in the hallway behind him switched on. He drew a knife from inside his leathers as he turned around. No one was there. Then a light went on across from the kitchen. Don Mars stood in silhouette.

"Kalan isn't here," he said slowly.

Don stepped forward, then walked slowly around the kitchen table, as did Vern.

"Bet you haven't seen one of these before," Don said, nodding toward the gun in his hand. "Have a seat."

Vern sat down slowly. He put his knife on the table.

"Put your hands on the table as well," Don requested.

"Who is Farlane?" Vern asked.

"I don't know what you're talking about," Don replied.

"I think you do..."

"Start paying attention," Don interrupted. "Do you know what this is?"

"It's a pretty big gun," Vern said quietly.

"See here," Don remarked while pointing to three letters etched into the enormous barrel after the number 390. "Any idea what HVS stands for?"

"No, I don't."

"High-velocity shot. That's what it stands for. This gun is an antique," Don said proudly. "Nothing better has come along since. Bullets launch out of the barrel at more than two thousand feet per second. Now you know. My dad got this over forty years ago. It's one of the first ones ever made. It even inspired me to be the fine marksman and weapons dealer that I am today. What do you think it's for?"

Vern just shrugged.

"You give up too easily. It was designed for huntin' big animals. Bear. Elk. Moose. It's probably just as good at nailing smaller critters too. Vermin, like you Mister Gedder."

Vern was visibly uncomfortable. "How do you know my name?"

"You need to learn how life in a small town works, Mister Gedder."

"You mean how life in this colony of clone freaks works," Vern retorted.

"The officer who pulled you over today knew something was wrong as soon as he saw you. He's the one who told me your name," Don said calmly.

Vern remained silent while Don looked him over for a few moments to size him up.

"On your feet," Don said.

Vern obliged.

"Walk real slow over to the front door. Keep your mouth shut too. Once your backside is on that porch I'm going to start counting to five. If any part of you is still on my property when I'm done I'm going to dust it."

Vern did the rough math. The location of his Renegade Alien. How fast he could run. How fast the bullet would travel. Physics were not on his side. He bolted into the darkness as fast as he could. Don started counting. Vern was lit only by random sheet lightning, his image was blurred by the heavy rainfall.

Each stride was a leap of desperation, knowing that his life could end any moment. He ran as if he was grasping the air ahead of him to find something to propel himself further each time his feet touched the ground. The more he slipped into the rain-soaked darkness, the harder it would be for Don to line him up for the shot. Vern sprinted with a raw determination brought on by sheer terror.

Don anchored his feet, leveled his shooting arm and trained the gun sight on Vern. It wouldn't be right to kill a man by shooting him in the back he thought to himself. A dead body on his property would be hard to explain, even for someone in the inner circle of Hadley's Crossing. If Vern got away unscathed he would presumably be back with reinforcements. Don's challenge was to injure Vern with a weapon that could blow him to pieces.

He took the shot through the veil of driving rain that was illuminated by flashes of lightning. Thunder boomed as the bullet tore across the top of Vern's left shoulder. The impact twisted Vern forward and threw him to the ground.

"Four," Don counted while setting up for another shot.

Sharp pain riddled Vern's left side. Shock forced the air out of his lungs. His left arm was useless to him whilst he lay at the far end of the lawn in a pool of water. He knew he had to forge on. He began hobbling desperately towards his motorcycle too afraid to look behind him.

Don fired a second shot. It severed a tree branch that crashed down across Vern's back. He yelled out in agony, but his cries were drowned out by the sounds of the storm. He crawled out from under the branch and into a ditch that ran beside the road where his motorbike was parked.

Vern scrambled deliriously along the ground to the far side of the bike, so as not to be easily visible to Don. He hauled himself onto the seat. Blood rushed down his arm. His back could barely take the weight of his body. He punched the touchpad a few times. The cockpit sensors guided the plastic casing to form around his body. The autopilot slowly reversed the bike away from Don's view. Vern struggled to put his mobile phone in the receptacle as he slipped in and out of consciousness.

Don could have shot Vern inside the cockpit of his motorcycle but chose not to.

Vern's Renegade Alien drove slowly back along the route it had taken earlier, with him slumped over crooked inside the cockpit. The computer searched for a destination. The indicator on the electric charge meter fell into the warning zone.

CHAPTER 7

Don Mars heard the inevitable knock at his front door the next morning. It still startled him, enough so that he spilled some of his coffee while he sat solemnly at the kitchen table. The Guardian always surfaced with frightening precision.

The two men made each other's acquaintance many years ago when the colony in Hadley's Crossing was young and fragile. Don was a new father in those days. He had accepted the responsibility of establishing a community of clones, in exchange for his son. The Guardian was hired to protect the colonies from any locals who became suspicious and asked too many probing questions. Don saw to it that they were relocated well before they discovered the town's secret.

The Guardian was a big man, with an intimidating demeanor. He let himself into Don's house as if it was his own. Don stood to his feet as he heard the footsteps approach. He had good reason to be wary.

"Has our close friend in whom we trusted betrayed us?"

"I have not," Don replied quietly.

"Did the intruder not find his way to you, the keeper of this colony, to commit violence against our people?" the Guardian asked.

"He came to harm my boy," Don said, fondling his revolver, to remind the Guardian who was in charge. "Where were you? You should have been here to protect us."

The Guardian said nothing.

"He is wounded," Don remarked. "He will lead us to those who sent him as he seeks their help."

"What then if he motivates others to come here to try and succeed where he failed?"

61

"That won't happen. He knows nothing about the colony. He's scared for his life."

The Guardian was dismissive. "If the colony is exposed people will betray one another. Innocent people will be slaughtered simply because they are different. Hatred will rule."

"You need to find him," Don said calmly. "I have done the work that you should have done. I have served him up for you. He could not have gone far."

"He has not shown up in the places that I would have expected," the Guardian replied. "Perhaps he is smarter, more prepared than you give him credit for."

"Patience," Don remarked. "He grows weaker with each passing moment. Time is working against him."

"It's too late," the Guardian replied. "Someone will come for you."

"You don't know that," Don scoffed. "You have become paranoid Guardian. Lax, even fearful. Just what the cults prefer. The colony faces adversity. This is the time to stand together, to rebuff this threat, yet you come to divide us."

"That is not my purpose," said the Guardian.

"We all know that Farlane is undecided. Should the colonies remain concealed, because we have been conditioned to live in fear, or should they be revealed because we are confident that they are strong enough to survive? Maybe it's time to take a stand."

"It is not our decision to make," the Guardian said quietly. "Whoever breathes out the secret of the colonies will atone for their transgression before me. Someone in this household revealed the secret."

"You are mistaken, Guardian. My boy knows nothing, I assure you. Have I not shown my loyalty?"

"Your dedication to the colony has always been exemplary. Which is why I don't understand why the zealot knew to come here. Farlane suspects that your success has inspired over-confidence and that you chose to test the cults. It is well known that you believe the colonies should be revealed. To show that the clones are normal people. You suffer from the misguided notion that if we tell the world that clones are alive and well they will be less stigmatized and publicly accepted."

"The first ones are old enough to have children of their own. The girl who grew up down by the corner will give birth soon. What does the Guardian propose?"

"You jump to conclusions about revealing the colonies. If the secret is kept, the clones will never know anything about Farlane. As the elders pass on, the secret will fade away and be taken to the grave. No harm will come to anyone."

"Are we to deprive young adults of knowing their true identity?"

"That is not a question that you and I have the authority to answer," replied the Guardian.

"Let us not waste time arguing over philosophy. I don't believe that anyone other than the zealot knows, or cares, one bit about Hadley's Crossing. Guardian, you must put him out of his misery and warn others who choose to follow him."

"They will find you," the Guardian replied. "Then they will break you."

"Why did you come here today?" Don asked.

"To tell you that you have to make a decision."

"Do I?" Don asked.

"You can choose to die in agony at the hands of a stranger, or you can choose to die with honor, in the colony that will immortalize you."

Don was silent as a look of disdain emerged on his face.

"I'm not here to kill you," said the Guardian. "I came to tell you that your death is imminent. There is nothing you or I can do to change that. It saddens me to bring you this news," he added somberly.

"I am less than impressed that you have come to thank me for my dedication in the manner that you have chosen," Don stated brusquely.

"What is your decision?"

"Go after the cults," Don replied. "Eradicate them. They are the problem, not me. You must not let them stigmatize the clones."

"What is your decision?" the Guardian asked again.

"You have become a disgrace to us Guardian," Don said as he pointed his revolver at the older man. Then he waved the barrel toward the door.

"Farewell Don Mars," the Guardian said as he walked down the hallway to the front door.

"I'll give your best wishes to Jane when she gets back," Don remarked defiantly.

"That won't be necessary," the Guardian replied. "I spoke with your lovely wife just before I came to see you. To pass on my condolences for her loss." The Guardian saw himself out.

Don walked outside the back of his house admiring the open country but enraged by what the Guardian had said. The strong breeze that blew the storm away in the night was dying down. He caught a glimpse of something moving off in the forest. Don stood up straighter to take a closer look. An arrow launched from a crossbow concealed amongst the trees confirmed the Guardian's prophecy.

CHAPTER 8

The desire for retribution in the face of flagrant betrayal was concealed masterfully amongst the trusted confidants. No one else who worked at the Wyndhall Life Sciences Research Centre had any reason to be alarmed about Don Mars' demise. Searches for the truths that govern the alteration of biological life continued to be conducted with the usual day-to-day introspective quiet steadiness, for appearances, despite the seething rage that burned within those with knowledge of the colonies. A furtive search for the perpetrators of treachery within this small community of brilliant minds had begun in silence.

Trent Carson stood at the apex of the biomechatronics laboratory. His arms were folded across his chest. His chin rested on one hand as he glared at the video wall that surrounded part of the curved platform.

"Rewind," he requested. "Go back to the beginning and then roll at ten times normal speed."

"Acknowledged," the computer replied, with a voice that could be mistaken for human. Microscopic images of cells dividing filled the transparent display that stretched from floor to ceiling. Three-dimensional graphics that tracked the time dependency of the molecular changes were displayed off to one side, just above the raw data signals. Trent watched as the cells divided and then grew into the neural interface organ.

"Stop," he requested. "Go back one-quarter of a second. Create a copy of that image."

"Acknowledged" the computer replied. A red light began flashing on the main console. "Doctor Wood is in the outer hallway, requesting access to this laboratory. She wants to speak with you. She says it is urgent."

"Access denied," Trent replied. "Don't let her in. She doesn't have clearance for this lab. Don't let anyone in. I need to work in peace."

"She is persisting," the computer remarked. "She says that her clearance has been upgraded."

"I didn't approve any request to change her clearance. Don't let her in."

Trent walked over to the control console in front of the climate controlled room that housed the reactors. He had meticulously programmed the computer to observe how the neural interface organ behaved when it connected a human brain to a computer. Motor neurons connected the organ to the stem of the brain. A robotic hand placed the signal ball, smaller than a marble, into the fleshy fold of the organ.

Once the transmitter turned on, wireless signals were sent to the ball. The organ converted the incoming information into action pulses which caused neurotransmitters to be released in the motor neurons. Electroencephalography showed the electrical activity in the brain. Trent watched in awe. "Add a sequence of these images to the file," he instructed the computer.

The preliminary results were encouraging enough for Trent to initiate a new experiment, one designed to grow a human fetus with the small neural interface organ, located behind one ear, connected to its brain.

Trent tucked his tablet computer inside his lab coat. He left to meet Sahil Mathai in the courtyard between the four buildings that comprised the research center.

"You survived the storm, I see," Sahil remarked to his younger protege.

"I lost power," Trent replied. "Some trees came down." Trent briefly took note of the woman who had entered the other end of the courtyard, patiently minding her own business.

"Did he tell you why it was so urgent to meet now?" Sahil asked.

"No. I thought he told you," Trent replied. "I can only assume that he wants to hear our news as soon as possible." He pulled out the tablet computer. "This is what I want to show him." He called up the digital imagery of the neural interface. "Proof that an organ can transmit information from a computer to a human brain."

Sahil took hold of the computer and stared intently at the images, then at the data showing the electrical activity in the brain.

"Welcome to the dawn of post-human evolution," Trent remarked calmly.

"Which chromosomes did you use?" Sahil asked.

'The first set that you prepared."

Sahil continued studying the image. "What should we name it?"

"Affinity," Trent proposed. "One with the world."

"That's it?"

"The expanded mind. Unity with artificial intelligence. Humans who will exchange digital information directly with computers," Trent added. "The boundaries of our imagination are about to be redefined."

"There must be a Nobel Prize in the offing," Sahil joked. "Trent Carson and Sahil Mathai creators of the new path to evolution."

"Don't get ahead of yourself," Trent remarked. "Let's see what Duncan says first."

"Did you start the next experiment?" Sahil asked quietly.

"Yes. Just before I came here to see you."

The two men walked back through the courtyard. "You and I have spent our working lives creating new life," said Sahil. "But what do we really know about the spirits we create? Ever think about their consciousness?"

"Good morning Doctor Mathai," the woman said politely.

"Hello Doctor Wood," Mathai replied. "I trust your visit with us is going well."

"Sahil, you go ahead," Trent remarked. "Tell Duncan that I'll be there in a few minutes." Sahil left the two alone and started making his way to a hastily called meeting with the Chief Scientist.

"Access denied?" Shannon Wood questioned playfully. "I thought my clearance was upgraded."

"The bio-mech labs are off limits," Trent replied. "Safety risks. Can't be too careful."

Shannon placed her hands on her hips, pushing open her long white lab coat. A tight-fitting dark dress revealed a stunning beauty that Trent lusted for. Her pose reprised one from late the night before last when Trent had accepted an invitation to join her for a dip in the luxury pool at her hotel. She slipped into the glassy water wearing a white lace bikini. Trent became enthralled by the touch of her lips on his as the couple basked privately in the liquid warmth under a starry sky. The sensuous touch of her soft skin fueled Trent's fantasy of seduction. Shannon was just as skilled at enticing Carson as she was at shying away from consummating his desires. She knew how to hold out for exactly what she wanted. Now Trent was a slave to satisfy his craving for her. "This is off limits to most people too," she said flirtatiously. "Your clearance is still upgraded. For now."

"I stopped by your hotel last night. Thought that we could pick up where we left off the night before..."

"I had other plans," she said in an aloof and nonchalant manner that stoked insecurity in Trent. "With some girlfriends," she added, to settle him down. "You and Sahil look like you are in a rush."

"Duncan called us in for an impromptu chat. Something is urgent."

"Don't let me make you late for something so important."

"Can I see you tonight?" he asked.

"I'm afraid not," Shannon replied shaking her head slightly. "Change of plans. I leave early this evening. I need to be back at the south campus tomorrow."

Trent saw the opportunity fading. His stalwart determination to uphold the security protocol of the bio-mech laboratory broke down as he succumbed to temptation. "Stop by my lab this afternoon," he insisted.

This was the breakthrough she had been holding out for. "I can't wait," Shannon replied with a smile. "I am sure that you will see to it that we are alone."

Trent left the courtyard to catch up with Sahil, who was waiting patiently inside the Chief Scientist's office.

"The battle for my succession has started," Duncan began dourly.

Sahil and Trent looked at each other. They were not here to discuss their recent work.

"How can you be sure?" Sahil asked.

"Don Mars is dead."

"Since when?" Sahil asked.

"Earlier this morning."

A heavy silence fell over the conversation, as the realization that a harsh reckoning would soon be at hand gripped the three men.

"Don was a good man," Sahil said quietly. He was visibly disturbed. "Was it one of us?"

"Can't be sure," Duncan replied. "Hard to imagine that either faction would gain anything by it. Whether you think that the identity of clones should remain hidden, or that society is ready to accept them shouldn't give one a motive to kill. This is a matter that must be settled with dialogue."

"Don believed that society is ready to accept the clones. That is not our direction at the moment," Sahil replied.

"That is precisely why I believe there is a challenge to my authority," Duncan said in a perturbed tone. "Don and I had philosophical differences, no doubt about it. We needed one person to start the first colony where clones could live peacefully, with protection. He stepped up to make that happen. His loyalty and determination were unmatched, which is why I believe he was so successful. He was murdered because of what he believed in. He was murdered to send the message that my time is up," Duncan concluded, pounding a fist on the table.

"There are only twenty of us spread across the three campuses," Sahil remarked. "It shouldn't be that hard to flush out each individual's intentions."

"I have that under control," Duncan replied dryly, provoked by the insinuation that he was not in tune with the opinions held within the group.

"Will Nisha be joining us?" Trent asked, somewhat perplexed.

"Two days ago Don's boy called home. His parents hadn't heard from him in months. Said he knew something about Damien Farlane. Yesterday he walked into a set up in the city. The guardian from Hadley's Crossing sent a bodyguard to protect him. The bodyguard didn't make it. He lived long enough to create a distraction. Nisha got Don's boy out. She took him to the safe house in Danor Township. Then the storm rolled in. No. Nisha will not be joining us today."

"How much does the boy know?" Sahil asked grimly.

"I spoke to him yesterday when he was at the safe house with Nisha. He knows that his identity is not what he was raised to believe. I don't think he knows the full truth. At least not yet."

Sahil thought for a moment. "Do we know how he found out?"

"No," Duncan replied.

"If one of the offspring knows enough to question their identity then..."

"It's just a matter of time until the others start to find out," Duncan concluded.

Grave concern showed on Sahil's face and in the way he spoke. "Kalan Mars must be isolated until we can find out what he knows. He needs to be convinced to keep the secret."

"That was my plan," Duncan remarked. "Kalan escaped from the safe house just before the storm rolled in yesterday. He can't have gone far. Nisha says she has the situation under control."

"Innocent people will be persecuted because of this," Sahil replied. "Modern society is still challenged to accept racial diversity and sexual preferences. It is not ready to accept clones as human beings. I don't believe any of us can imagine how quickly the fear of clones could be spread in this post-truth culture we live in."

"It's worse than you think Sahil," Trent asserted. "People will question their own identity. Social media will whip that up into a firestorm. Panic will ensue. That is the threat that the perpetrator is counting on to get what he or she wants. Change leadership now and the threat goes away. Don't change leadership and the secret will be revealed."

"The science that our group is dedicated to has to be practiced with the greatest of confidentiality. If I understand the membership correctly, maintaining our perpetual veil of secrecy has spawned a form of oppression," Duncan remarked. "We live in a free society. Yet we are held captive by the results of our work to further human enhancement. This continues to be the hypocrisy with which we must live, for now. The free world isn't ready to accept our best discoveries, in spite of the benefits they bring. Unassisted evolution ended over a decade ago. Creating human babies with mitochondrial transfer using DNA from multiple people has been around for over ten years. It is widely accepted. Yet, we cannot share our main work within the broad community of scientists for fear of reprisal from those scientists who don't support human enhancement. Add to that the psychosis brought on by these secret societies who have chosen to politicize science as evil, in order to advance their agendas. That is the burden that we all knew we would carry when we signed on to this project. There will come a time when society will welcome the work that we have done. Better to divulge our secrets then, instead of caving to pressure and wreaking havoc now."

"Who do you think killed Don Mars?" Sahil asked Duncan.

"I suspect that we have been infiltrated," Duncan replied angrily. "That's why I requested this meeting. If an organization like the Society for the Elimination of Artificial People knew of Don Mars' role in the life of Hadley's Crossing then they also knew that killing him would start the process of revealing the secret."

Trent and Sahil looked at each other with dismay.

"Watch your backs, gentlemen," Duncan warned. "Who you trust may be your undoing."

XXXX

Shannon Wood watched Sahil and Trent leave Duncan's office from behind a corner at the other end of the hall. A moment later she knocked twice on the door, then let herself in as planned.

"You seem stressed," she remarked.

"Not more than usual," Duncan replied.

"Your heart rate is erratic. Your blood pressure is elevated. Your electrodermal activity suggests that you are highly agitated, perhaps even nervous. Your brain waves are close to maximum frequency. Something has disturbed you."

"I don't think we need a diagnosis of my physiology at the moment," Duncan replied dryly. "Let's get on with reviewing your report."

"Where would you like to start," Shannon asked as Duncan opened her report on his computer.

"I read your findings with great interest. They are, in one word, complicated."

"In what way?"

"They raise questions about loyalty that I had not expected."

"Does that observation apply to the whole group or just certain individuals?" Shannon asked.

"You tell me," said Duncan.

"The group seems to accept the cover that you set up for me: an immunologist working on contract who attends each campus on a rotating basis to study the health of their laboratory specimens. This group of scientists has two populations. The longer-term members are motivated by a sense of purpose. Some of the newer members are driven by personal ambition. Their membership is simply a platform for them to launch their careers, in spite of what they tell you. Nisha Lin is the one whose loyalty to the group is most in question."

"That seems hard to believe," Duncan remarked.

"She tries too hard to fit in," said Shannon. "Whenever the two of us meet her biometric responses show that she is agitated, possibly nervous. I can't be sure of her intentions."

"Perhaps you simply have not spent enough time with her," Duncan remarked.

"My findings are only qualitative," Shannon reminded Duncan. "They are limited because my questions are incidental perhaps even social in nature since the main topic of my interaction with the group is the health of their specimens."

"Your extrasensory skills," Duncan remarked, "seem quantitative enough."

"You must be careful when interpreting that information," Shannon replied, "as random error is relatively high. I only see the group members intermittently. There are no controls on the observations that I make. I have no sensory baseline for each member to compare to."

"Perhaps your observations about Nisha can be explained by personal chemistry, or the lack of it. Maybe you just don't like each other," Duncan suggested.

"Are you proposing that my assessment of Nisha is rooted in a dislike for her?" Shannon asked.

"I admire her skill to think creatively. Her courage to fight for truth is exemplary. Nisha has an edge to her. She can be vain at times. That bothers some people. Makes her somewhat of an outsider. I suspect that she may regard you with envy. You are more accepted within the group."

"I highly doubt that," Shannon replied coolly, seeing an opportunity to change the subject. "Why do you only want me to work with such a small group of scientists?" she asked.

"I have my reasons," Duncan replied.

"Do you know that two of the microbiologists on the south campus, outside of the group of twenty scientists that you asked me to work with, are agents for the Society for the Elimination of Artificial People?"

"They are only passive agents," Duncan noted with some disdain. "They are not invasive, or actively looking for secrets to disclose. They are just doing their jobs."

"You don't seem concerned."

"Their presence adds a certain complexity to how we manage information at the south campus. But that facility is dedicated to therapeutic studies, not our more controversial work. We can tolerate this pair for now."

"I have nothing else to report," Shannon concluded. "Do you have any further questions?"

"No, I don't," Duncan replied. "You have been most helpful."

Duncan stood pensively looking out of the window in his office, shrewdly pondering his next move when Shannon entered the airlock of the bio-mechatronic laboratory on the floor below. Once the glass door locked behind her, air from the jets above swirled softly downward through her long dark hair. She stood alone in the chamber, eager to see what was concealed behind the interlocked steel door just beyond the glass door in front of her. The powerful whir of air flowing from the jets by her sides suddenly kicked in. The wind blew furiously like a tornado throughout the tiny chamber. Her hair was tossed in all directions. Her lab coat blew open, her dress fluttered around her thighs. The rush of air stopped almost as suddenly as it started. The bolts recessed from the door in front of her. It swung open with an uncanny silence as if to invite her to step onto a small mat situated in front of a lens.

"Good afternoon Doctor Wood," a computerized voice said after the facial recognition scan was complete.

The steel doors in front of her opened slowly. Shannon walked into a secret world where new building blocks of biological life were expanding the possibilities of human definition.

"This way," Trent beckoned from the platform in the middle of the laboratory. Shannon looked windswept, from her encounter at the entrance, yet she was even more attractive to Trent.

"At last. The mystical bio-mech lab," she remarked while glancing around as she walked toward him.

"What makes this place so mystical?" Trent asked in a serious tone.

"It actually looks genuine," she quipped. "With all of the security around here, you would have the perfect cover for a boys' club. You, Sahil, Duncan all the guys. I expected to come in here and find the world's largest golf simulator."

Trent wasn't sure how to respond to an attempt at humor from someone who was typically only serious.

Shannon could sense that he was eager to carry on from where they left off in the pool the night before last. His heart rate was increasing. His arteries were dilating.

"It's hot in here," she said as she walked up to the platform. When she reached the top it became clear to her why this was such a secretive place.

A collection of smaller laboratories were recessed deep into the ground. Reactors of many descriptions were shrouded with sensors and cameras. Computers on the platform provided all of the details about the creatures that were forming under Trent's watch. She ran her fingers through her hair to recompose herself.

"I guess I'm used to the temperature in here," Trent replied.

"It won't break any protocols if I take this off will it?" Shannon asked as she fanned herself with the lapels of her lab coat.

"No," Trent replied. "Better?" he inquired, once Shannon had draped her lab coat over a chair, to reveal her slender figure in a sleeveless dark knit dress.

"A little better," she answered. "What's this?" she asked while pointing to one of the video images.

Trent struggled to maintain his composure. "That is the electrical activity of the human brain."

"How about this?" Shannon asked as she looked at the screen with great interest.

Trent stood behind her and put his hands on her hips. "This is a more sophisticated experiment," he said. "The reactor is an artificial womb." Trent reached over her shoulder to touch the magnified image. "On this side you can see an egg in this small chamber. Over here you can see the pool of gametes. Seed, that will be shot into the chamber in a few minutes, once the conditions are just right."

Shannon turned around and looked into Trent's eyes. She stepped closer so that her body touched his. Your reactor is getting excited is what you are saying," she remarked.

"I had not thought of it that way."

"It's still a little warm in here," Shannon purred. She reached beneath her dress then delicately stepped out of her red tanga panties. "That's better," she said. "How about you Trent? Are you getting excited? I sense that you are." She guided his hand to the zipper. Seconds later her dress slipped to the floor.

CHAPTER 9

Kalan crouched down, exhausted, against a tree trunk to watch the safe house from the cover of a dense thicket. Suspense gripped him as he braced for another encounter with Dagger Lady and her gang. He watched for any movement that would reveal the position of those who had been in close pursuit throughout the night. Patience was in his nature, but he was running low on energy. He needed to find food.

There were no voices nearby. Only a tenuous silence that was periodically disturbed by the rustling of leaves in the trees. Lack of sleep and the stress of being hunted had blurred Kalan's senses. He shuffled through the tiny opening in the bush. The safe house was empty.

Broken glass littered the kitchen floor. A couple of pot roaches had been left on the table, near a half-empty forty ouncer. Kunai swords were lodged firmly into the bullet hole ridden door that led out one side of the house. Blood dripped down the door and pooled on the floor.

Kalan rummaged around Dagger Lady's room, then the bathroom. Luck was on his side. A bottle of rubbing alcohol was next to the soap beside the sink. The sharp sting on his leg shook off his lethargy. His fall the night before, at the edge of the ravine above Hawthorn Creek, had opened a gash down one of his legs. Once a bandage was secure Kalan looked around for supplies. Two slices of stale bread were all he could find. He devoured them quickly.

"Scape" was handwritten on the label of a small package of tiny purple pills on Dagger Lady's night table. The recreational drug of choice in this part of the country was known for instilling a powerful feeling of invincibility. Gangs commonly used it to prepare for conflict. Scape was also renowned for unleashing raging sexual desire. Stains on the unmade bed were the first clues.

Judging by the lone used condom one man must have reached the safe house before the rest. Kalan surmised that the sex was over well before the other three men arrived. He figured that all of the men had partied with Dagger Lady as they crafted a plan to track him down. They must have smoked up, downed some of the gin and then sampled the Scape. Their pursuit of Kalan was likely delayed when something set off the Dagger Lady.

Glasses had been thrown indiscriminately. One man tried to rush out the side door. A barrage of the Dagger Lady's swords almost pinned him to the door. One of the men hit him with a shotgun blast, but he managed to crawl away into the night.

XXXX

Kalan peered out of the window in the cedar cabin near the old cemetery as the storm raged outside. He knew they would come for him under the cover of darkness. Soon after the rain let up he caught glimpses of beacons off in the distance moving slowly through the bush. The lights went out just before they reached the clearing that led from the forest to the cemetery. Kalan slipped out of the cabin and found refuge behind a small woodshed nearby, to wait apprehensively for the inevitable encounter. Wisps of fog swirled through the cemetery. Dagger Lady and her stoned clan suddenly appeared, like apparitions who had just risen from the dead.

"Die clone," the big man yelled out as he drew his gun and kicked the cabin door open.

"Don't kill him," another man yelled. "We need him alive."

The big man refused to be told what to do. His accomplice drew his gun and fired first. Dagger Lady retrenched to the side of the cabin, away from the shooting. The big man fell to his knees, turned and fired back. The accomplice was hit, but he squeezed off one more shot. Silence. Dagger Lady stepped forward and peered into the cabin. Both men lay dead on the ground. The cabin was empty.

"He must be alive when we do the test," she told the one man who remained. "He's still on the run. We have to find him."

Kalan backed away slowly through the forest towards the ledge high above the river to escape from his pursuers. He just needed to climb down the first few feet of a steep rocky slope to take shelter beneath the craggy overhang then disappear down the path near the top of the ravine. He slipped on the wet ground and tumbled over some sharp rocks before crashing into a tree. It broke his fall, but the noise gave away his position.

Kalan heard someone running towards him. He tried to crawl under the ledge to seek cover, but his stalker reached the ravine first. Kalan froze. The man looked around cautiously in the dark. Kalan aimed his Silent Destroyer towards the shadowy figure. His nemesis slipped in and out of view as the clouds let glimpses of moonlight through. Footsteps drew closer to the small bush where Kalan was taking cover. He fired a few pulses off into the darkness. The high energy shots were invisible to the human eye.

Dagger Lady's accomplice yelled out. She stepped unknowingly within inches of Kalan as she took cover behind some bushes.

"I'm hit," he said, writhing on the wet ground.

Dagger Lady looked around to try and discern where the shot came from. The man managed to stand up and limp towards the ledge. "The shot came from over there," he pointed. Kalan fired again. The man's cries faded as he fell toward the river below.

Dagger Lady rushed to where the man last stood. It was too late. Kalan had already made his way to the path at the top of the ravine and disappeared into the night. She walked back to the small cabin and fell asleep on the dingy cot.

XXXX

Kalan picked up the package of Scape to look it over once more. When he put the drugs back on the dresser he inadvertently knocked over a small lamp. The base of the lamp was hollow. He was too young to recognize the old style high definition transmitter. He crushed it anyway. Now Kalan was even more convinced that this place was a trap, in spite of being called a safe house. He stepped out of Dagger Lady's room to follow the blood-spattered footsteps of the man who had fled out the side door.

Rain from the storm had washed some of the tracks away in the night, but they were still visible enough. It was not long before Kalan came across a Kunai sword lying on the ground covered in blood. Judging by the impressions in the dirt the man collapsed here.

Kalan followed the cryptic hand prints that grasped for one more yard and the smear from a leg that could no longer walk that was dragged through the dirt, as the man struggled to get to the main road. A few minutes later Kalan came across the corpse.

Buckshot riddled the man's back. Kalan patted him down. The dead man wasn't carrying much. A locked smartphone was the real treasure. Kalan swiped the phone over one of the dead man's index fingers. Luck was on his side.

He ordered the robot car as fast as he could. Then he pulled out his pistol. The dead man's index finger remained rigidly in place, on account of rigor mortis.

Kalan used his Silent Destroyer to severe it off at the first knuckle. Then he made his way to the main road.

Dagger Lady crashed hard in the night. By the time she dragged herself back to the safe house, Kalan was long gone. She knew that a reckoning with Duncan would come soon.

XXXX

Raging winds hurtled sheets of rain in the path of Vern Gedder's Renegade Alien. The auto-navigation system was taxed even further while it rapidly searched for a hideaway. The wind blew the bike from side to side. Vern laid unconscious on the carbon fiber bike frame. Power drawn by the gyroscopic stabilizers drained even more charge from the batteries as they fought to keep the bike upright. Vern and his motorcycle were running out of time.

The computational search engine set coordinates for a farm in the hills beyond the town limits. The headlights switched off. The bike rolled slowly over the dirt and stones of the unpaved laneway while it quietly made its way into the storage shed. The batteries were almost drained. A Renegade Alien looked oddly at home hidden behind a mighty Lone Harvester autonomous tractor. This place was isolated. There was a power source that worked with Vern's motorcycle. The survival search criteria had been met. A small red indicator on the control panel faded. The bike switched into sleep mode.

Vern awoke slowly the next morning. Savagely growling Rottweilers in the night seemed like a vague memory. He could not explain why he was resting comfortably on his back in a strange bed.

A matronly woman knocked on the door jamb before letting herself into the room.

"Where am I?" Vern asked.

"Rolling Meadows Farm," the woman replied.

Vern sat up in the bed.

"Doesn't that hurt?" she asked.

"It's not bad. I should be on my way."

"Hogan wants a few words with you before you leave," she said. "You sure that doesn't hurt?"

"I'll be fine. How did I get here?" he asked.

"Beats me," the woman replied. "The storm was whippin' up all kinds of fury. Suddenly the dogs took off barking like maniacs. Next thing I knew, Hogan carried you upstairs and asked me to patch you up."

"You some kind of doctor?" Vern asked.

"My name is Millie, thank you for asking. I serve as the vet here on the farm." She sat down at the bottom of the bed.

"Well, Millie my name is..."

"I already know your name Vern. Hogan can get into that with you. Hold your arm up," she said.

"I'll be," she remarked. "Straighten it out and then hold it up higher."

Vern obliged.

"Holy Mother of... I ain't never seen anything like it. You on medication?"

"No," Vern replied, shaking his head.

"Someone took a shot at you that's for sure. That biking jacket packed some serious protection. It deflected a lot of the damage. Perhaps more than I thought. You were a mess last night. Today you're better than I expected."

"Lucky for me," Vern replied, not knowing what else to say.

"There's a bathroom across the hall. Come on downstairs for some breakfast when you're ready."

Vern emerged a few minutes later.

"Go ahead," said Millie. "Take a seat."

A hearty breakfast was laid out on the table. Suddenly a shot fired from a high power rifle. "Damn spy drones," someone cussed. A second shot rang out from the porch at the front of the farmhouse.

An older man entered the kitchen. A long grey beard grew out of the wrinkles that were chiseled into his face. Thick woolly hair flowed down over his broad shoulders to his biceps, which were as big as small tree trunks.

"I like desperate men, Vern Gedder," the man remarked. "I like desperate men because they will do desperate deeds."

"Hogan, I take it?" Vern asked.

"That's right," the wily farmer replied. "Dig in. No point letting any of this wonderful grub get cold," he said.

"How do you know my name?" Vern asked.

"You're a popular man," Hogan answered. "Just after daybreak one of the cops from Hadley's Crossing showed up. Said he was going door-to-door looking for a young man. Then he pulled out your picture. About an hour after that the Emperor of Hadley's Crossing himself showed up asking if I knew anything about a young man who had been shot last night."

"Emperor? I don't get it," Vern remarked.

"I don't like politics Mister Gedder," Hogan remarked. "You're not from around these parts, so you probably don't care for a lengthy description of the social strata. This guy called the Guardian oversees the pecking order over there."

"Is he the one who protects the clones?" Vern asked.

Hogan looked over at Millie. "Maybe you know more than I gave you credit for," Hogan replied.

"Mister Gedder's wounds are healing faster than I thought," said Millie.

"Wonderful news," Hogan declared.

"Thank you for taking me in last night," Vern said, trying to read the intentions of his hosts.

"No, no," Hogan replied. "Thank you for choosing us to be the ones to help you in your time of need."

Vern looked perplexed. "What do you farm here?" he asked Hogan.

"Sanity," Hogan replied. He started to laugh at the confused look on Vern's face.

"We pride ourselves on our dairy cows," Millie added. "We keep a small herd of hogs. Some chickens as well."

"One thing about these parts Mister Gedder is that more people are dying or moving away than are being born or moving in," Hogan remarked. "People don't usually take much notice of what happens around here. That's the sanity part. Makes it easy to live off the land and avoid the chaos that is called modern society, where everybody is watching everybody. People got no respect for anyone else's point of view. No privacy at all, not to mention these damn spy drones that showed up this morning."

"You said something about desperate deeds."

"Seems like you know a little about Hadley's Crossing. Smart folks can keep secrets in these remote parts if they put a little effort into it," said Hogan. "We've got a little secret here at Rolling Meadows. Ever seen this before?" Hogan asked as he produced a small packet of tiny purple pills.

Vern shook his head. "What is that?"

"Escape," Hogan replied. "Except the locals are lazy so they call it "Scape" for short."

"What is it?"

"Mind alteration candy that gives you a trip like nothing else," Hogan boasted.

"So this is your secret?" Vern asked.

"Technically, it's Millie's secret. She invented it," Hogan replied. "Haven't been able to get decent medicine for our animals for ages, so Millie concocted her own painkiller. Then we got a little more creative. You can buy cheap copies, but she still is the only person who really knows how to make it."

Vern sat back in his chair. "What's the deal?"

"You got no place to go. Powerful people are looking for you. Did I mention the reward they're offering?" Hogan teased. "It's just business. I can turn you in and make a small amount of money. Or, you can make a delivery for me and I'll make way more money. You can either be their captive or take a shot at remaining free. That sound like a deal to you?"

"What's the catch?" Vern asked solemnly.

"There ain't no catch," he replied.

"Hogan," Millie said, raising her eyebrows.

"Well there's no real catch," Hogan qualified. "Think of it as your chance to set a personal best. I need you to go a small town called Brawer. It's about forty miles due north from Hadley's Crossing. Last time one of my regular couriers rode up there he never came back."

"So, my personal best will be making this delivery alive," Vern said.

"Precisely," Hogan replied.

Vern sat quietly for a moment.

"There's something else that might interest you," Millie added. "I heard that people started gathering around Brawer a couple of days ago. I can't say that I know why, but I have a hunch that it has something to do with what's going on in Hadley's Crossing."

"The cop who stopped by this morning mentioned that a resident of Hadley's Crossing named Don Mars shot an intruder last night," said Hogan. "The Guardian informed us that Don was killed early this morning. I figure that you're the guy who paid Mister Mars a visit. The people you will be delivering this to might turn out to be kindred spirits."

Vern was intrigued. He looked over at the package that Millie had put down on the table. The small box covered in some brown paper had a small tracking device taped firmly to one side, with a tiny flashing blue light.

"What's that worth?" he asked Hogan.

"A fiver," Hogan replied with a smile.

"Thousand?"

"Hundred thousand," Hogan clarified.

"I ain't got much choice, do I?"

"Not really," said Hogan. "When you make the drop some of that scratch will be yours. I'll fix you up with a map that bypasses the place where the last runner disappeared. You'll depart through the woods just behind the shed where your bike is. The route will avoid the areas where the cops fly those damn drones. You'll be fine."

"Don't the bandits in these parts just figure out the frequency of your tracking signal then jack whoever has the package?" Vern asked. "Turn off the tracker," Vern remarked. "Then I'll do it."

Hogan stared at him, looking perturbed. "I'm not going to let you walk out of here carrying that kind of stash without..."

Vern interrupted. "How do I know that you won't have someone hijack me right before the drop just to avoid paying up?"

"I could call the officer who was here earlier," Hogan remarked.

"Hogan, you need to back down a little," Millie insisted.

"Here's what I'll do," Hogan said, after thinking for a moment. "I'll disable the tracker, but not the timer."

"How will that protect your stash?" Vern asked.

"The guy you give this package to will answer that question," Hogan replied.

Millie sat down. She reached out and took one of Vern's hands then held one of Hogan's hands. "Let us pray."

CHAPTER 10

Vern walked his motorcycle the short distance over to the edge of the trees on Hogan's land. Staying upright on dusty trails, navigating swamps and weaving through forests over rolling countryside would all be tough challenges for a Renegade Alien. It was not designed for that type of riding. The race against time began, but the motorcycle struggled to maintain balance and slowed down. Vern had no choice but to press on. He had a destination to reach on a deadline. Kalan Mars did not.

XXXX

Kalan traveled north towards Hadley's Crossing late that morning. He leaned against the window in a drowsy state, lost in thought. He plugged his Silent Destroyer into one of the outlets, then dozed off. The robot car braked hard to a full stop as it came out of a sharp bend at the base of a steep slope. Three men stood boldly in the middle of the open road. Two of them brandished rusty metal pipes the size of baseball bats. The man in the middle brandished a long knife. He motioned for Kalan to get out.

"I want to look inside your car," the man said as the others laughed ghoulishly.

Kalan calmly stepped away from the car onto the shoulder beside the road. "It's not my car," he remarked.

Bandits, who trolled the desolate countryside, were common in Red Zones, like this one. This group ventured away from their small collection of makeshift cabins in the woods to hijack whatever they could from traffic on this back road. Leaving the safety of the forest to commit robbery in broad daylight was a risk they had to take. Times were tough. Their faces had a rugged appearance that was as menacing as it was desperate.

"There's nothin' here," the man with the knife hollered. His scraggly beard and unwashed look accompanied a foul stench that was overbearing. "Make it easy," he said to Kalan. He stepped closer. "Give us whatever you can. We're just looking for something to help us get by."

"I don't have anything to give you," Kalan said as he sized up the two men who brandished the pipes. "I'm as desperate as you guys are."

"I know you," the man said in a gruff voice as he pointed his knife towards Kalan.

Kalan looked into his eyes. Gerald Huff looked much older and more gaunt than he should have. The abrasive bully who once tormented Kalan as a teenager was reprised as a poor man.

"You made it out," Gerald said enviously noting that Kalan seemed to have made a life in the world outside of Hadley's Crossing.

"Huff, you're still just a punk. If I need to humiliate you one more time in front of your fellow losers then hurry up and get it over with."

"Let's take it to him boys" Huff said as his gang moved in.

Branches at the tops of the trees suddenly swayed vigorously, despite the stillness in the air. Huff's gang looked up perplexed by a buzzing sound that grew louder. A prototype of the new Civilian Menace drone emerged from its invisibility shroud, locked onto the distress signal that was transmitted from the car.

Huff's gang feigned calmness in the face of this robot officer of the peace. Nothing about the drone gave any indication that it was empowered to make decisions about how to deliver justice. The machine quickly determined who the perpetrators were. Three smaller drones fell away from the main body, then swooped down to within a couple of feet of the men in Huff's gang. Each one darted and dashed with ease as they circled the men, taking pictures at will. Small canisters of pepper spray and nine-millimeter guns were locked onto Huff's gang all the while.

"You are free to go," a robot voice told Kalan.

He wasted no time returning to the car.

The men in the gang backed away slowly hoping to return to the forest. One of the small drones got too close for comfort to Huff's lieutenant. He swung at it with his pipe, but the agile drone swerved, barely avoiding the shattering blow. It shot a burst of pepper spray to fend the man off. Then the small drones flew back and reintegrated with the main body for safety.

Huff and his men took advantage of the momentary break. They bolted frantically toward the cover of the forest.

The drone slowly descended further. One twelve millimeter gun deployed from the bottom. The men made it the edge of the woods. Just before they disappeared into the foliage three laser-guided shots broke the tense silence. The drone slipped back into invisibility mode to move on to the next distress call. Kalan was long gone.

XXXX

Lost Ridge Lodge dated back to well before Kalan's time. This majestic old hotel drew people to the remote serenity of Blue Opal Lake for years. He came here as a young boy with his parents. Kalan stepped out of the car. He stood still for a few moments and relived his happier memories of this place when he explored the trails, fished in the lake and roasted marshmallows over campfires at sunset. The lodge looked very different now.

Shutters hung precariously from some of the windows. The rot had crept along the wood railing on the spacious balcony on the second floor. Many of the cabins looked like they had been taken over by forest people. The front steps were cracked, covered in weeds. Kalan stepped inside, into a run-down version of the ornate lobby he had grown fond of as a boy. Stones that made up the giant fireplace were covered in soot. Oak planks in the floors were warped and loose. Initials were hacked into the mighty cedar beams. Stuffing crept out of rips in the grand leather couches. Particle board covered the openings where skylights in the cathedral ceiling used to brighten the whole room. A gamey odor hung in the air. The main restaurant was still in service.

"You look hungry," the man behind the counter remarked.

"What's good today?" Kalan asked.

"Burgers," the man replied.

"Sure," Kalan remarked. "What's in them?"

"Mostly deer. Some groundhog. A few other critters as well."

"That's all you got?"

"That's all we got," the man replied. "Do you want one or two?"

"One will be enough."

"How are you gonna pay?"

Kalan pulled an electronic token out of his pocket.

"You want to use money?" the man asked, looking disappointed.

"What did you expect?"

The man leaned forward. "I was hoping that you had some Scape," he whispered.

"Afraid not," Kalan replied.

"Then it's gonna cost you a little more."

Kalan sighed.

"The hotel business here isn't what it used to be. A woman bought the rest of my supply a couple of days ago," the man said as he passed Kalan's order to the cook. "Demand seems to be up. I'm just trying to make a living."

"Sure."

"Been here before?" the man asked.

"Must be at least fifteen years ago," Kalan remarked.

The man thought for a moment. "Those were the good days," he said. "It wasn't long after when people started moving out of the towns and into the forest in these parts."

"Looks like they've taken over."

"Everybody around here adjusted their expectations," the man replied. "Permanent work that used be found nearby is mostly gone. Living as a prepper ain't nothin' to be ashamed of."

Kalan couldn't get that phrase out of his head later in the day as he closed in on Hadley's Crossing. He decided against calling in advance. Better to show up unannounced and deal with Don spontaneously. Kalan pulled the dead man's finger out of his pocket, then brushed it across the scanner to pay for the ride.

He stepped out of the car. It disappeared down a side street while Kalan walked down the road to the house he grew up in, preparing for the inevitable conflict. The lights were out. The front door was locked. Kalan stood on the landing wondering what to do next.

"No one is home," an old woman called from across the street. "The gathering is at the inn."

Kalan walked through the old neighborhood. He climbed the small hill that led to the inn wondering what gathering the woman was referring to.

Older people slowly filed into the building. They looked forlorn. Kalan wondered what tragedy had struck the community. He recognized many of them as the parents of the families that came to see Don from time to time when he was a boy. They didn't know what to say to Kalan when he appeared to be unaware of the situation.

The Guardian stood solemnly beside the entrance. Jane Mars stood off to one side at front of the central hall. Kalan made his way through the small crowd. Once he grew closer he could tell that she was stricken with grief. When Jane first saw Kalan she was in disbelief. She looked up at him with tears in her eyes then hugged him.

A tall slender man dressed in a black suit walked into the main hall from a side door. He asked the visitors for their attention. His associate slowly pushed the open casket into the main hall. Don Mars looked as stern in death as he looked in life.

Kalan was taken aback, horrified to see the dead body of his father. He instinctively helped Jane sit down on one of the folding chairs that had been set out throughout the room. He was overcome with confusion and despair.

"Be seated," the man in the black suit requested.

The Guardian closed the doors at the back of the main hall to stand watch over the visitation. He looked over the room. Meyers was the one man who was missing. The Guardian understood why. He gave the nod to begin. Members of the small gathering listened stoically as Garvan Maynor, the man wearing the black suit, spoke.

"Don Mars was taken from us too early. Tonight we celebrate his courage and dedication to serving our community," he said. The man paused to look down at the lifeless body in the casket for a moment. "Recall his wisdom when conflict finds you. Be inspired by his resolve to face adversity. Remember his commitment and sense of responsibility. Keep his memory alive in your hearts." He invited the mourners to rise and say a few words.

Don Mars' closest confidants stood up one after another. Monument to integrity. Role model. Inspiration. Once the last tribute had been given, the man in the black suit motioned for all to rise for a moment of silence before inviting them to come and pay their respects.

A line formed as the people slowly filed by the casket. A few of the men slipped off to one side.

"What are you hearing?" one man asked quietly.

"Fear has gripped the families," another man added. "No one knows what to do next." He nodded slightly towards Kalan, who was standing across the room. "The Guardian figures that someone labeled him for being a clone."

"How did they know that?"

The man shrugged. "No idea."

"Some guy came to hunt him down, but Don fought him off. That's what I heard."

"I heard the same thing. No one can tell me if the guy he fought off is the guy who killed him."

"Don had a few enemies. Families who had to be silenced. Back in the early days. I figure that one of them carried a grudge. Never got over it. They waited until Don least expected it."

"I'm not so sure," one of the men said. "For all we know all of our children have been identified if the Guardian is right."

Garvan Maynor joined the conversation. "Is it true?" one of the men asked.

"Is what true?"

"The rumor that people are assembling in Brawer before coming to reveal the clone families in Hadley's Crossing," the man replied.

"How do they plan to do that if they don't know which families in Hadley's Crossing are clone families?" another man asked.

"I heard that the Guardian is ready to make a deal."

"Let me handle the rumors about Brawer," Garvan replied calmly. He pointed toward Kalan. "We need to get him away from here. Until this all blows over. Which one of you can shelter him for a few weeks?"

The men looked at each other. "I'll do it," one of them finally replied.

Garvan approached Kalan. He put one hand on Kalan's shoulder. "I can't imagine how difficult this is for you," he said. "You have my sincerest condolences."

Garvan's solace came across as contrived to Kalan. "Why did someone do this?" Kalan asked with a puzzled look. "Why did they kill my father?"

"I don't know," Garvan answered.

Kalan backed away. He sensed that the people paying their respects to his father privately held him responsible for his father's death.

"I know a safe place that you can stay for a while," Garvan remarked.

"A safe place?" Kalan questioned.

"I'm trying to help you," Garvan insisted.

Kalan's mother appeared overwhelmed. She had little time to speak with him during the visitation. Kalan had to choose between the offer of safety or disappearing to fend for himself. He backed away from Garvan. He turned to leave the main hall, but the Guardian stood between him and the door.

"Get out of the way old man," Kalan said.

"Can't do that," the Guardian replied as he stood his ground. "Tell me what you know about our secret. We are here tonight because of you."

Kalan discreetly pulled out his Silent Destroyer and held it close to his side. He knew that the Guardian could tell that the weapon was fully charged. At close range, a single shot would blast right through him. The Guardian looked sternly at Kalan, then stepped aside. Kalan took one look back at his mother, before walking briskly out of the inn.

He pulled the dead man's stiffened finger out of his pocket one last time. The stranger's mobile phone came to life. The call to Devon Granger was brief. Kalan needed to know where they could meet.

Don Mars' visitation lasted long after Kalan disappeared into the night. People across the street stared with interest.

"What is your secret society hiding?" one heckler yelled.

The mourners paid little attention as they left the inn. The Guardian quickly summoned his henchmen to reign the crowd in. Garvan stepped aside and took a call. He was hesitant to believe Meyers at his word. Then someone threw a bottle stuffed with a lit rag from beneath the trees. The bottle shattered and burst into flames close to where Jane was walking. Garvan changed his mind. He granted the approval that Meyers sought. Garvan was all in.

XXXX

Jane was surrounded by friends when there was a knock at her front door. A woman who was new to the neighborhood asked to come in and pay her respects.

"I don't know why the man wouldn't let me join the visitation," she remarked. "These are for you." She handed Jane a small bouquet of lilies and gladioli. "My deepest sympathies."

Jane Mars thanked the woman, then invited her to join the conversation.

"I sense the division here in Hadley's Crossing," the woman remarked. "It's like there are two communities. But I don't understand why."

"Perhaps we can discuss that another time," one of the women proposed quietly as she held out a tray of hors-d'oeuvres.

XXXX

Vern drove up to the office at the junkyard in Brawer after dark. A tower of lights shone down on the twisted heaps of metal. Motors churned loudly. An old car rose slowly above the fence line tethered to a giant magnet. Then it stopped. The man behind the controls stepped outside.

"You're late," the long-haired man told Vern. "Give me that package," he demanded.

Vern handed him the scape.

"You're lucky that Hogan didn't hit the button."

"The timer is automatic," Vern replied.

The man unwrapped the package. "See that. It's an explosive charge. Doesn't matter if the timer is automatic or not. If Hogan thinks a shipment is lost he blows it up." The man switched the controller for the explosive off.

"How much time did I have left?" Vern asked.

"Less than two minutes," the man replied. "What took you so long anyway?"

Vern rolled his eyes. The man stared at Vern's bike.

"That is an impressive machine. I guess a Renegade Alien ain't really built for riding trails," he remarked.

"Or crossing streams, or driving through mud," Vern added.

"Wait here."

Moments later a tall man with a mustache came to see Vern.

"This is for you," he said handing Vern a wad of cash. "We could have done them all at once if you got here sooner," he barked at Vern.

"What are you talking about?" Vern asked with attitude.

"Hadley's Crossing, that's what I'm talking about. The whole brain trust was in the same place tonight. I could have roasted all of them at once. Except I had to wait on your lazy ass to bring me the Scape."

"Stone sent you here, didn't he?"

The man went silent for a moment. "You know Stone?"

"I met him once," Vern replied.

"Walk with me," the man said.

Vern walked his bike alongside the man on the short trip from the junkyard to the small house at the edge of the hamlet.

"We're going to get high," the man remarked. "My boys like to be high when they go on a rampage. We're going to tear up Hadley's Crossing."

He walked ahead of Vern, who stepped away to park his bike alongside a large pine tree. A small dart hit Vern in the neck. He was being carried away when the explosion blew the first floor of the house out sideways. Moments later a second explosion blew upwards, once the top of the house collapsed down on top of the occupants. A fireball launched high into the night sky. Meyers and his small crew walked out of the woods to finish off anyone who may have survived the blasts. The man who walked with Vern laid motionless on the lawn in front of the house. One of the crew got up close to him, then emptied his clip. Just to make sure.

Meyers and his men drove away from Brawer, leaving the house to burn.

CHAPTER 11

The early morning sun shone through the frosted sky-lights above the biomechatronics laboratory, illuminating the pods with a red glow. Duncan and Sahil patiently inspected the data on the screens beside each of the artificial wombs in the warmth of the hatchery. Tubes carrying the fluids that brought life to the embryos pulsed rhythmically in time with the heart beats. Tiny cameras recorded every movement. Sahil paused briefly from his clinical work to enjoy a rare sentimental moment.

He had devised the neuroscience and genetic sequencing that brought the attributes of a genius' brain to the embryos in the pods. An enlarged corpus callosum would allow more complete connection between nerve fibers in both hemispheres. Increased power of thought processes would be achieved with intensified columns in the frontal cortex. Controlled length of the connections in the cerebral cortex would permit intense focus on the singular subject matter, or broader thinking to evaluate larger problems from new perspectives. Reduced dopamine receptors in the thalamus would enable unconventional solutions to challenges that average human brains disregard. Strengthened parietal lobes would allow specialized skills to be developed quickly.

He marveled at his creations. These embryos would be born with the most advanced minds that biology could achieve. They were the last ones. The final generation of human clones that Sahil would bring to life.

Mozart's string quartet in D minor began playing softly. The ovoid pods moved slowly in the dimness. Sahil followed Duncan to the womb off to one side, where the embryo with one of the advanced brains and the affinity organ grew inconspicuously.

"Won't be long now," Duncan said confidently.

"I wish it could be me," Sahil mused. "A mind connected to all of the knowledge humankind has created and continues to create. It would be glorious."

"The human mind merged with machine intelligence," Duncan remarked. "Well before it was believed to be possible."

"But will it be too late?"

"Why do you ask?"

"You and I stand proudly here today, at the dawn of affinity. But we both know the day will come when humans will no longer be masters of the Earth," Sahil remarked. "We will be overtaken by AI for good."

"Scalability is humanity's defense," Duncan remarked. "If the first affinity child proves viable we could produce millions of them every year."

"How do you propose that society will integrate millions of new affinity children every year?" Sahil questioned.

Duncan sensed the frustration in his old colleague.

"What are you hearing about Brawer last night?" Sahil asked as the two men stepped out of their clean suits in the room beyond the airlock that led to the hatchery.

"I did not want it to come to this," Duncan replied quietly.

"We did it?" Sahil inquired.

Duncan did not like the inference of responsibility. "What the colonies do to maintain peace is their business, not ours," he replied. "Garvan Maynor, the new protector of Hadley's Crossing, seems to be more accepting of the Guardian's extreme methods than Don Mars was."

"I heard that Brawer was a staging point. The Society for the Elimination of Artificial People were ready to storm into Hadley's Crossing to expose the clone families."

"That's one story," said Duncan. "Another story is that a large amount of Scape was sold in Brawer last night. The deal fell apart. There was a fight. The drug house went up in flames."

"You made decisions without our involvement," Sahil complained. "If SEAP has the ability to identify clones how long will it be before they come after us?"

"SEAP is fighting those who are pushing to lift the restrictions that prohibit human-form robots from being integrated freely within the population," Duncan replied. "I sense that they assumed a quick victory was theirs for the taking at Hadley's Crossing. It would have boosted their public profile. They won't make that mistake twice."

"What makes you so sure?" Sahil asked in a tone that suggested he was losing confidence in Duncan.

"Garvan took a hostage last night," Duncan replied. "Someone that SEAP will want to be returned. We're in control at the moment. I'll see to it that Stone leaves us alone once and for all. When the time is right."

"It's not safe to do this work anymore," Sahil said. "I want out."

"You can't get out now," Duncan replied, pointing back towards the hatchery.

"Sometimes you lose sight of who you are talking to," Sahil chided. "You should think deeply and move slowly. Right now your actions are not rational."

"The new embryos need you. The rest of the group needs you," Duncan said.

"It's not about the group anymore. It's about staying alive. The younger scientists are ready. Their time to lead has come. You want to take a bullet for the cause, that's your business," Sahil retorted angrily. "Right now, my ego is satisfied. I've done enough."

"Where will you go?" Duncan asked.

"I'll figure something out," Sahil replied.

"Where else will you find the freedom to pursue the science of human enhancement in a setting where your results are delivered directly into society?"

Sahil walked over and looked into the hatchery.

"You exemplify the inner conflict experienced by everyone in our small group. Modifying human biology in secret while cultivating the public image of an esteemed researcher who publishes what the scientific literature judges as ethically acceptable."

"What's wrong with that?" Sahil asked. "The results that I publish accelerate the treatment of illnesses that afflict many humans. Don't forget that I used to be a leading practitioner in the field of genetic modification for approved purposes."

"The results from conventional research rarely get into the population," Duncan said dismissively. "Cures never materialize. Clinical trials become overwhelmed by bureaucracy. Not to mention indecision caused by ethics and regulations. It is not in you to tolerate restrictions. We both know that you won't last a week in any other research center."

"I chose this path because I believe that working to enhance human life is a worthy cause," Sahil said at last. "Humans can be better than machines, not slaves to them. Doesn't mean I'm ready to die for it."

"Be careful what you decide," Duncan remarked. "Until the mole in our midst has been exposed."

XXXX

Hugo Melling sat slumped over in a large armchair. His limbs were limp. His head drooped over one side of his chest. Drool seeped slowly out of his mouth down the bib that Doctor Lin's assistant placed on him. The bandage that used to conceal where the affinity organ was surgically attached to his skull, behind his left ear, had been removed.

Hugo opened his eyes. His empty gaze soon gave way to concentration. Nisha adjusted the signals. Hugo sat up, in complete control of his body.

"How are you this morning, Hugo?" Nisha asked quietly.

He moved his mouth awkwardly, but could not make a sound.

"Try it now," she remarked.

"Better," Hugo replied in a deep, slow voice.

"Do you feel up to walking?"

Hugo placed one arm on each side of the chair. He struggled to pull himself to his feet. Nisha made the necessary modifications. Hugo stood up and walked slowly from one end of the room to the other. "How am I doing?" he asked.

"Fine," Nisha replied. "Just fine." She began the next phase of the therapy. "Hugo, I want you to answer some questions for me."

Hugo stared stone-faced through the thick plexiglass.

"What is your full name?"

"Hugo Randolph Melling."

"How old are you?"

"Thirty-nine."

Nisha took a moment to confer with her assistant.

"Why am I here?" Hugo asked.

"You were injured in an explosion," Nisha replied.

"What is your name?"

"Nisha."

"How long have I been here, Nisha?"

"Almost one year," Nisha replied. She began to introduce data from the Internet into the affinity ball. "You were brought here after your condition stabilized at the trauma center where you were taken after the incident."

"Where is here?"

"Wyndhall Life Sciences Research Centre," Nisha replied. "Based on the severity of your injuries you were a candidate for advanced brain reconstruction."

"I have no recollection of coming here," Hugo replied.

"That was by design. We kept you sedated until the healing process was complete."

Hugo slowly put his hands on his head. He lightly felt around, searching for scars from the surgeries. "What is this?" he asked as he felt the extra thick layers of skin behind his left ear.

"A new organ," Nisha explained. "Inside the extra skin between your earlobe and where your ear attaches to your skull are millions of new neural connections to your brain. I tucked a tiny ball inside that new fold of skin right beside your skull. It is the size of a small marble. The ball contacts your new neural pathways. It receives wireless signals from the device attached to your belt. It converts those signals into electrical pulses that stimulate your brain."

"Really?" Hugo marveled.

"Yes. That ball has enabled your brain to function again. Its power to exchange information with your brain will only increase over time. I started sending you signals from the Internet a few moments ago. Can you tell?"

Hugo felt his memory begin to return to what he thought was normal. "I think so. Is that because of the ball?"

"Yes," Nisha replied.

"What if I lose the ball?" Hugo asked with concern.

"We'll simply get you a replacement," Nisha answered. "I need you to keep what you know about the ball a secret."

"Why is that?" Hugo asked.

"It is new technology. Some people are nervous about new things, especially when they are as powerful as that ball. What if someone used it to control you, to make you do bad things?"

"That scares me," Hugo said nervously.

"I didn't mean to scare you. I wanted to point out why we must be discreet about what you are learning today."

"I won't tell anyone."

"Good," Nisha replied. "Where were we? The data you are receiving relates to your case. What were you doing just before the accident?"

Hugo spoke very slowly and deliberately as the thoughts and images unfolded in his mind. "I was walking down the street. I saw the sign for the cafe. A man suddenly ran out of the door. He collided with me and I fell down. The mask he wore became dislodged, just for a brief moment. After a few second, I stood up and took a step. My memory is blank after that."

"Can you hold an image of the man's face in your mind for a few moments?" Nisha asked.

"I will try," Hugo obliged.

Nisha nodded to her assistant, who then instructed the computer. A picture of the man who bombed the cafe appeared on the screen. "It's not much to go on, but it's the best that I can get," the assistant said to Nisha

"Hugo, are you tired?" Nisha asked. "We have one last exercise on our list for you today."

"It depends. What is it?"

"Calibration therapy. We will provide your brain with instructions for something it has never done before. We will monitor you and make adjustments as your nervous system carries out the instructions."

"What am I to do?" he asked.

"Take a seat at the piano on the other side of the room."

"I have never played the piano in my life."

"That's the point," Nisha replied.

Hugo closed his eyes and grimaced at first. His fingers stretched to reach the keyboard. His clumsily plodded through the first few bars. It gradually became easier for him, as the smile on his face indicated. He stopped. "I don't know that tune," he remarked.

"That will be enough for today," Nisha said. "Hugo, without the affinity ball you will revert back into the comatose state that we revived you from. My assistant will take you to a special apartment that we have prepared for you in one of the faculty residences. She will explain the plans for the rest of your rehabilitation with us."

Nisha went to her office after leaving the rehabilitation center. Calibrating Hugo provided her with a new understanding of how much information a human brain could receive and share with computers. She was on the threshold of a breakthrough.

Nisha reviewed the electronic traces from Hugo's affinity organ meticulously. Switching efficiency was higher than her calculations predicted. When the DNA nano-machines in the affinity organ relaxed they unfolded and contacted the surface of the affinity ball. When the nano-machines folded, the connections to the affinity ball were broken. Digital switching of wireless signals by DNA at the speed required to process thoughts in a human brain was confirmed.

Her demeanor appeared calm, but her nerves were tense in anticipation of Duncan's arrival. Duncan was still ruffled from his encounter with Sahil. His expression suggested that an inquisition was imminent

"Why did you let him go?" Duncan asked pointedly.

"Why did I let who go?" she replied.

"Don't play games," Duncan said. "Kalan Mars. What happened at the safe house?"

"I didn't let him go," Nisha answered. "He escaped."

"Escaped?" Duncan asked. "We agreed that you would hold him there into the evening so that we could move him under the cover of darkness."

"So why didn't they show up?"

"You tell me," said Duncan.

"What's that supposed to mean?" she asked.

"The Guardian said he would send four men."

"He only sent one," Nisha scoffed.

"Who was it?"

"They never tell you their names. The hot one with the big muscles, covered in tattoos. He came late. Kalan was gone."

Duncan looked agitated.

"Kalan was well armed. He packed a Silent Destroyer. I did the best I could to keep him in the safe house. The Guardian's muscle man showed up just after Kalan disappeared. After the storm hit, three more men showed up."

"Who were they?"

"How should I know?" Nisha asked rhetorically. "I'm lucky that Kalan was gone by then. If he had been there we would have had a fight on our hands. The only reason I'm alive is that they needed me to help them find Kalan."

"Why should I believe that?" Duncan asked. "What if the real story is that Kalan was going to be handed over to SEAP from the moment you got him into that car? When those who came for him didn't find Kalan at the safe house, the deal fell through and the fighting started."

Nisha cursed. "That's ridiculous."

Duncan backed down. "I'm not saying that you were responsible. I'm saying that you may have been used."

"Was that your plan?" Nisha asked in return.

Duncan glared at her.

"So you needed to show someone else that you were willing to put me in harm's way. Is that what you are saying? Who do you owe?"

Duncan grew infuriated. "I need to know who is loyal and who is trying to push me out..."

"I put myself in considerable danger for the group," Nisha interrupted. "Now you are insinuating that I am disloyal. How do I know that I wasn't set up? I got Kalan out of the city. I took precautions to make sure that we weren't followed. Why did you rely on the Guardian at Hadley's Crossing for protection? Why didn't you send some of our people?" Nisha was angry.

Duncan pondered his response. "This institution must survive as the people who serve it come and go. It must create the environment for those who are driven to explore human enhancement while working in secret. I make the decisions necessary to preserve that," he remarked.

"You have lost your edge," Nisha interrupted. "You are the one who has put the group at risk. Not because of what you choose to do. Because of what you choose not to do. Or don't have the balls to do."

A look of shock appeared on Duncan's face.

"Affinity technology has tremendous value," Nisha stated. "A human organ that connects a brain to the Internet will command considerable power and money. Clones are a mere stepping stone in that journey. The collective body of work that the group is exploring has become too big for one person to manage. You are starting to screw up."

"I resent that accusation," Duncan replied.

"We both resent some of the accusations today," Nisha replied.

Duncan looked away, towards one of the large information screens in Nisha's office. "Lost my edge," he repeated slowly.

"Perhaps you have been compromised."

"By what?"

"Greed and power," Nisha replied. "Can any of us trust you in your current state of mind?"

Duncan glared at her once more, then left.

Nisha settled back into her work. She pulled up the image. Paula Slate, Nisha's assistant, returned from escorting Hugo to his apartment. "Perfect timing," she said. "This was created from the information we extracted from Hugo's mind early this morning."

Paula looked at the image closely. "This is the man who evaded capture for bombing a cafe in Haven City Number Two?"

"Let's call it in."

"Can't do that," Nisha said. "Whoever you call it in to will ask where it came from. We can't reveal that."

"So let's call it in anonymously," Paula suggested.

"Too risky," Nisha replied. "The trail will come back to us."

Her assistant held her head in her hands.

"Are you alright?" Nisha asked.

"I don't know. I'm not sure," Paula replied. She took a moment to breathe deeply and collect her thoughts. "We have created the means for the contents of a human mind to be hacked," she said.

"You must not think of it that way," Nisha said reassuringly. She placed her arm on her assistant's shoulder for encouragement. "Take a look at the traces that we measured from Hugo..."

Paula stepped away. "You don't get it," she said.

Nisha had never seen Paula act like this before.

"I'm sorry," Paula said. "We are not just enhancing humans. We are making it possible to invade and alter the individuality and memory of every person. This is bigger than any of us can understand. It can't be right." She fled from Nisha's office distraught by what she had helped to create, frightened by what would happen if it was not stopped.

CHAPTER 12

"It's the waiting that gets to me," said the first spotter. He lit another cigarette.

"You need to get into the right frame of mind," Devon replied calmly. "Be patient."

"We're wasting our time here. If that Inspector was for real he would have called by now. I think it's a setup."

"I told him that we weren't going to wait forever. He's got another couple of days. Give him credit for the digs," Devon remarked gesturing to the surroundings in their luxury apartment.

"We need to find Kalan," the first spotter said. "So that we can get out of here and get back to making money."

"I'm all for that," the second spotter added. "We're like sitting ducks cooped up in here. I don't like it."

"The Inspector seems convinced that Birchstone is still under threat. Something about more targets here being valuable. Says that's why he is footing the bill for us to stick around."

"Bet he hasn't said what those targets are. How can we prepare if we don't know..."

Devon checked the call display before answering the Inspector's call. "Twenty minutes. Where?"

XXXX

Devon watched the bird of prey swoop closely past his shoulder. A single unsuspecting crow had flown deep into the falcon's territory. The falcon flew in behind the intruder, determined to track its frantic darting and swerving.

"It's like the work that we do," the Inspector remarked as he stood beside Devon on the path in River Park. Birchstone sprawled peacefully in the valley below. "The trick is knowing when to pounce."

No maneuver in the crow's repertoire could save it. Once the falcon's sharp talons gripped the crow firmly, it launched into a dive. It released the crow just above the rocky outcropping near the path. The crow tumbled helplessly along the hard surface, coming to rest in a lifeless heap. The falcon swerved, then landed beside it. A tomcat poked out of a nearby shrub to see if the fallen bird would be an easy meal. The falcon had a challenger.

The cat crept out of the shrub, hunched down, ready to stalk the crow. The falcon chose to avoid a confrontation with the cat and flew away. The cat raced towards the crow at full speed.

The injured bird mustered the will to hobble before lifting off the ground. The crow's wings faltered, and could not give it enough altitude. The cat took a swipe with one of its paws. It clipped the crow's tail feathers, knocking the bird back to earth. The beleaguered bird struggled to get up. The cat pounced, clamping its teeth down hard on the helpless crow's neck. The bird struggled less and less as the cat hauled it away into the solitude of the shrub.

Devon pondered what the Inspector had said. "Your work is like that of the cat. But you don't know how to disrupt an invader and prepare it to be finished off. That is because you have not adapted your methods to understand how and where people who detest Red Zones will strike. My work is like that of the falcon," Devon said. "The cat would have missed a meal if it were not for the falcon."

"I have a tip about another attack," the Inspector remarked.

"What's the target?"

"Best not to speak about it openly," the Inspector said, ignoring Devon's question.

"Your people should be able to handle it now. You don't need us," said Devon.

"We shouldn't have needed you a few days ago. Turns out that the force had enough information, but no one acted."

"That surprises you?" Devon asked.

"The force has been infiltrated," the Inspector muttered. "I'm sure of it."

"The longer we stay here, the more we risk having our cover blown," Devon said.

"I need to explore all of my options," the Inspector replied. "Enlisting your group and paying you a bounty is one option."

"Preventative arrests. Autonomous drones. They're better options."

"You're not listening. I need the force to approve pre-arrests. I need to request autonomous drones from the force. If the force has been infiltrated, who am I going to trust?"

"I get it," Devon answered. "Our group is less hassle, maybe even expendable..."

"Preventative arrests are on the way out, even in Red Zones like this one. Can't get convictions anymore, not even from die-hard law and order judges. Autonomous drones work well in rural areas, but they leave too much collateral damage in urban areas, like Birchstone."

"I wonder what target could be so valuable?" Devon inquired.

"There is some urgency," the Inspector revealed.

"Tomorrow?"

"Day after tomorrow. Is that yes or no?" the Inspector asked.

"We'll do it. For five times as much as last time."

"Five times..."

"Sounds like we're the only option you have. For immediate assistance," Devon remarked. "I need some of it now."

"Just in this for the money," the Inspector remarked shaking his head.

"Quite the opposite," Devon said confidently. "I know how to put a fair price on the task that you are signing us up for."

The Inspector selected the icon on his mobile phone. "How much to sign you up?" he asked.

"Forty thousand," Devon answered.

The Inspector handed Devon his phone to key in the password and account information.

"I wish you success on this assignment," the Inspector remarked.

"Where do we have to be and when?"

The Inspector handed Devon a folded piece of paper. "This has all the information that you need."

Devon opened the note briefly then slipped it into a pocket. "Paper? Is this all you've got?"

"Aren't you going to read it?"

"I saw enough. I'll read the details later." Devon remarked. "The lads and I are obliged to you for not blowing our cover. And for the place to stay."

"There is another matter that we need to discuss before you leave," the inspector replied.

Devon looked surprised. "What?"

"That man standing over by the fountain. He witnessed the shooting. He wants to speak to you."

"Are you out of your mind?" Devon gasped.

"Keep it together," the Inspector said calmly. "I've convinced him not to disclose what he saw. He'll keep it that way so long as he gets to speak with you."

"What if I don't want to meet him?"

"Says that he has information that could save your life," the Inspector said before he walked away.

Devon was curious and approached the man.

"You were in the park during the shooting," the man remarked. "I saw you."

"The Inspector didn't tell me your name."

"You may call me Stone," the man said.

"The Inspector said that you are bound to keep what you know about the shooting quiet," said Devon.

"That's right," Stone replied. "I have nothing to gain by bringing attention to an event that the Inspector wants to remain covered up."

"Why should I believe that?" Devon asked bluntly.

"You should not waste your energy thinking about me," Stone replied calmly. "You have humiliated the Inspector."

"Is that what he told you?" Devon asked.

"Police in this Red Zone enforce law and order any way they see fit. I don't think they are thrilled about being outsmarted by a bunch of amateurs. My guess is that he's looking for revenge, even though his chief ordered him to work with you."

"What do you want with me? I don't have much time."

"You were with a man who looks remarkably like a man I know."

"You used whatever connection you have with the Inspector just to tell me that," Devon taunted.

"You think that what I have come to tell you is not important?" Stone asked.

"What do I need to know about this man?"

"He hunts down human replicas," Stone replied.

"Or shoots at people that he thinks are human replicas," Devon countered.

"Exuberance is a weakness that he has yet to grow out of," Stone conceded. "May I suggest that your weakness is that you take the uniqueness of your persona for granted."

"I have other things that I need to do." Devon started to walk away.

"What makes you so sure of your identity?" Stone asked as he grasped Devon's arm.

Devon grabbed Stone's throat. "Hands off," he said quietly. He glanced back up the hill at the spotters, then shook his head slightly. "You don't want to find out if someone in the trees behind us is prepared to dust you, do you?"

Stone let go of Devon then backed off. He could not see the two men who had methodically targeted him from the camouflaged vantage point on the hill. "I'm not going to call your bluff," Stone replied. "You can choose not to know what I know if you wish."

"Make it short," said Devon.

"Your friend's double has proof that small towns scattered across some of the Blue Zones have housed human clones for years. These places have allowed replicas to integrate themselves into their general populations," Stone stated. "I think that your friend comes from one of those towns."

Devon paused. His family had moved to Hadley's Crossing to welcome a sister into the fold. "You're saying that my friend is some kind of freak?"

"No, not at all," Stone replied. "Quite the opposite. I suspect that your friend is enhanced in many respects. He is certainly not a freak. He is likely stronger. Smarter. More capable in many ways than the rest of us."

"Why would you be concerned about someone who is enhanced, as you call it?"

"The real danger is that over time they will become the masters of humanity. They will command all of the resources, all of the opportunities. Others will be pushed to the margins of society."

"You think that is grounds to kill someone?"

Stone did not answer Devon's question. "That fear drives some people to do such a thing."

"I'll take that as a yes," Devon replied.

"People would be irate if their true identity was proven to differ from the identity they grew up with," Stone remarked. "Humans cannot be their own creator."

"People would have to care first," said Devon.

"That is easy to say now," Stone remarked. "No one has any reason to consider that clones walk freely in society. Visceral fear of the unknown will spread rampantly once the news gets out. Forget about rational thinking. Paranoia will sink in. Chaos will prevail."

"Sounds pretty dramatic. What's in it for you if chaos is averted?" Devon asked.

"Nothing. I want this to end peacefully," said Stone. "Those who are enhanced must be identified. The practice must be stopped. We will find a way for those who are enhanced to live out their lives without jeopardizing the human race."

"What do you want from me?"

"I want to help you," Stone remarked. "You are in danger. Once your friend chooses to exercise his strengths you will not be able to stop him. He trusts you, which gives you the advantage. Contain the situation while you can. Before more violence breaks out."

"You said something about what you know."

"Clones were a great experiment, thirty years ago," said Stone. "The science was reasonably strong, based on experience with other mammals. Breakthroughs in artificial organ technology were made regularly. You could dream up practically any genetic sequence, e-mail it to the right 3D printer and create a new organism in a few hours. The temptation to enhance humans appealed to a minority of scientists who felt that laws and regulations inhibited scientific progress."

"You were there?"

"Yes. Long enough to see the early failures. Infants who were deformed. Young children afflicted with the illnesses common to clones of other mammals. Much more effort went into computer simulations of the biological and physiological outcomes. The results provided a path forward so that human clones could live into adulthood. There was a catch. The simulations predicted that severe mental disorders would become a possibility once the clones reached their mid-twenties."

"What kind of disorders?"

"Violent dementia," Stone replied.

"Only a possibility you say," Devon remarked. "You want me to hand him over to you. The Inspector wants to go public with the shooting, but you will hold him off as long as I do what you want."

"I could think in those primitive transactional terms," Stone said. "But I don't need to. Your friend will need help. When that time comes you will need someone to call." Stone held out his mobile phone. "I will be available to help when the time comes."

Devon transferred Stone's contact information to his phone. "I don't need your number, in case you're wondering," Stone remarked. "It's better this way. You need to know who I am. That's all that matters between us."

"Not what I expected," Devon said.

"Your friend has likely found refuge in one of the Blue Zones," Stone surmised. "Tolerance and support for his condition will be abundant if he finds the right people. I don't like the divisions that we live with. Red Zones, where society is more controlled. order. Blue Zones, where society is less ordered. Rational thinking will be overpowered by irrational violence unless tact and intelligence are applied. Just because I reside in a place as extreme as this Red Zone does not mean I would be any less predisposed to help you."

"The way I see it Red Zones are where people's rights are diminished at the hands of demagogues. People can't speak freely for fear of attack. Blue Zones are where freedom is still practiced, for now," Devon replied. He looked over to where the Inspector was standing. "If you really want to help, walk with me over to those trees. I'm going to take off. Kindly maintain the appearance that we are still having a conversation."

A couple of minutes later the Inspector strolled down the path towards Stone. "Where did he go?"

"He slipped away," Stone remarked. "I was speaking to him one moment, the next minute he was gone."

XXXX

"Crossing out of this Red Zone won't be easy tonight," the first spotter remarked. "Make sure that your mobile devices are turned off."

"Can't this thing go any faster?" Devon whined as the robot car drove along the solitary country road.

"You can get out and push if you like. What did the Inspector want?" the second spotter asked.

"To set us up," Devon said.

"You don't buy it?" the first spotter said as he handed the piece of paper from the Inspector back to Devon.

"It doesn't add up."

"What do we do now?" the first spotter asked. "There is the old covered bridge."

"Approaching Blue Zone," said the computerized voice in the car.

"Stop here," said Devon.

The car came to rest in front of a clearing in the trees.

"Full moon tonight," Devon noted.

"We're at least thirty miles from Hadley's Crossing," said the second spotter.

"We're not going to Hadley's Crossing," Devon said. "Once we cross that bridge we'll pick up another car just down the road. We won't have far to travel after that."

"I reckon that bridge is only about a hundred feet long," the first spotter remarked.

"One hundred feet. That's all that separates repression and freedom," said Devon. "Rotating border closures are in effect. Mandatory detention of people at border crossings is enforced here. Looks like we are in for some fun."

"There is nothing around here for miles except open country," the first spotter remarked. "Why would someone build a covered bridge here?"

"To keep you dry as you cross the river," the second spotter replied, in jest.

The first spotter positioned the car to within a few yards of the bridge. It rolled slowly down the road as the men bolted away from the bridge and down the embankment in search of a place to cross the shallow river. Once the car disappeared into the bridge the sound of a metal gate closing with a mighty clang broke the silence. Drones that shone lights on the entrance soon appeared over the Red Zone side of the bridge. A border patrol officer drove up moments later. He drew his weapon, then proceeded to see what was in the trap.

Devon and the two spotters crossed over a pathway of rocks in the river. Once they were on the other side they ran through the fields to the car that was waiting for them.

"Destination reached," the voice in the car said, twenty minutes later.

The first spotter knocked on the door of the deserted cabin. Kalan recognized the code.

"You look well," Kalan said to Devon and the spotters.

"You look worn out," Devon replied as he embraced his friend. The spotters followed suit. "It's good to see you."

"Quite a place you have here," the first spotter remarked sarcastically.

"Could be worse," Kalan replied.

"What is going on?" Devon asked.

"Some say I am a human replica. The guy who tried to shoot me believes it. Medical records infer it. Hadley's Crossing is a place where clones are raised in secret." Kalan sounded as frenzied as he appeared. "They killed my father. Why would they do that?"

"I don't know," Devon answered. "I'm sorry to hear that." He paused for a moment. "Have you heard of a man called Stone? He says that clones of your age lose it. Go berserk. Snap. Says that he was involved with cloning humans. Says the science isn't right."

"You believe him? You think I am a clone?"

"I don't know what to believe."

"People are becoming paranoid. They will brand me as suspicious, even as an enemy, just because they think I am different."

"We're all tired," Devon said. "Let's get some rest."

"Can you contact this man Stone?"

"Yeah," Devon replied. "He might be able to help you."

Kalan looked tired but showed resolve. "We will settle this in the morning."

CHAPTER 13

Paula Slate cased the space. She walked slowly through the hatchery early that morning. She stopped in front of the pod with the embryo that was destined to grow into the first human with an affinity organ. Her decision was final. She knew precisely how to terminate the embryo in a way that would imply failed cell division.

"Isn't this supposed to be Doctor Carson's shift?"

Paula was startled. She turned to find Doctor Wood standing right behind her. "We switched shifts," she replied nervously.

Doctor Wood eyed Paula closely. She could sense deception, even through the assistant's sealed body suit.

"I didn't know that you had permission to enter the hatchery," Paula said, as she composed herself.

"Perhaps you would like to check with Duncan," Doctor Wood said, to distract her. "To put your mind at ease," she added reassuringly.

Paula exited the computer menu that controlled the pod, frustrated that completing her task would need to wait.

"Let's get a coffee," Doctor Wood proposed as they walked through the main hallway after leaving the hatchery. "Duncan won't be here for at least another half hour."

"Alright," Paula replied cautiously. "I need to stop by my office for a moment. I'll join you soon."

Doctor Wood touched Paula's wrist gently. It was a friendly gesture. "I'll find us a place by the window."

XXXX

Devon woke to find Kalan sitting on a chair staring out of the front window of the one-room cabin. "You look stressed out," he remarked warily.

"See that?" Kalan asked.

"See what?"

"Another drone flew past. That's the fourth one in the last hour. What did you guys do to set them off?"

"What makes you think they are looking for us?"

"You think they are looking for me?" Kalan asked. "Because I am some freak that must be captured before I wreak havoc on society."

"We were set up," Devon replied. "The lads and I got out just in the nick of time."

"We need to get out of here."

"To go where?"

"To a place where I can find out who I really am," Kalan said.

"That sounds ambitious, under the circumstances. Let's get you some help. How long has it been since you ate something?"

"Where do you propose that I go? I can't show my face anywhere. My picture will be posted all over the Internet. If I turn my phone on someone will pinpoint my location and come for me. That's the world I live in," he said as he kicked an old floor lamp.

Devon could sense that Kalan's anger had peaked. "I get it. You are in a tough place, but you're losing it. I want to call this guy Stone. You seem to think someone else can settle this. Which one of us makes the call?"

Kalan walked over to his jacket, uneasy that Devon was suspicious of his every move. He pulled out his mobile, turned it on and dialed.

XXXX

It was odd for Nisha to find the lights on in her laboratory. She was usually the first one to arrive each morning. "Paula?" she inquired. No response. Nisha stepped forward then noticed someone lying face down, motionless on the floor. She rushed to the woman. No breathing. No pulse. Nisha gently rolled her assistant onto her side. Her eyes looked blankly at Nisha. A blue hue of death was spreading across her face.

Medics from the Central Care Unit arrived moments later. Resuscitation proved futile. The first responders somberly wheeled the stretcher away, after exhausting all possibilities for revival.

"Do we need to lock down?" the medic team leader asked with urgency.

Nisha was stunned, distracted with gloom.

"Doctor Lin," the medic said assertively. "Do we need to lock down?"

"I can't imagine...," Nisha mumbled slowly to herself. "Have you responded to any other incidents in the complex this morning?" she asked the medic.

"No. We need to report this to local police." the medic insisted.

"Work that out with Duncan," Nisha said. "Find out what killed her. I want updates every fifteen minutes," she told the medic. "We can't have outsiders investigating this place looking for answers."

"What was going on in here?" the medic asked.

"Nothing that should have killed anyone," Nisha replied. "I'll have the security video checked for the entire complex. Meet me here in an hour and a half."

Nisha locked her laboratory. She cautiously made her way to the main security office, looking for clues as she walked through the complex. "What have you found?" she asked, without checking to see who made the call.

"Dagger Lady, there isn't much time."

"Kalan?"

"I figure that you know who Stone is. You want me alive. He wants me dead. He is probably already on his way to kill me. You need to move fast."

"Where are you?"

"Where I will be is what concerns you. Check the co-ordinates after this call." The line went dead.

Nisha picked up her pace.

"Good Morning Doctor Lin," the man managing the main security desk said.

"Normally I would ask to speak with Vaktol. It seems to be too early."

"Yes, it is," the security guard replied.

"What time did Paula Slate arrive this morning?"

"We don't just give out information randomly," the man replied. "You need to file a request."

"I understand," Nisha replied. "She reports to me. I am entitled to ask a few questions confidentially if I understand the procedures correctly."

"Is there a problem?"

Nisha hid her knowledge of the circumstances. "You're the one who will have the problem," she said glaring at him. "Vaktol won't want to find out that you interfered when I tried to address an attendance matter with someone on my staff."

The security guard relented. "Paula Slate. Building pass accepted at 5:56 AM. The door to your laboratory opened at 6:09 AM. Entry to the hatchery at 6:14 AM. Exit from the hatchery 6:21 AM. Satisfied?"

"What happened after 6:21 AM?" Nisha asked.

"I don't know," the security guard replied.

"Check the video. It's only eight minutes after 7:00 AM," she added.

The security manager isolated the video feeds. "Not much to see here. Paula suits up. Goes into the hatchery. Comes out of the hatchery. Doctor Wood comes out a few seconds later. Then Paula scanned into your lab."

126

Nisha looked confused. She did not have the luxury of time to think through all of the details. "Put Doctor Wood in supervised patient isolation. On my orders. Tell her it's for her own protection. Make sure that your men don't let her touch them. She may be infectious."

"Doesn't the medic team make that decision?"

"Just do it," Nisha insisted. "I need to attend to something urgent. Tell Vaktol that I will call him as soon as I can."

Nisha called the medic as she raced towards the garage under the complex. "What killed her?"

"It's only been fourteen minutes..."

"I need answers sooner."

"We don't know for sure," the medic replied. "A stroke, a brain aneurysm..."

"Have you completed a physical examination?" Nisha questioned.

"Not yet."

"Call me as soon as you have answers."

XXXX

"Destination in twenty-one minutes thirty seconds," the robot voice in the car said. Nisha sat pensively as the vehicle took her to the location that Kalan's phone had provided. When would she make the call? "Destination in twelve minutes," said the voice. Still too soon. "Destination in three minutes."

"Vaktol," Nisha said. "Have your men tracked her down yet?"

"Calm down," a deep voice replied. "What is going on?"

"I don't know," Nisha replied. "My assistant died shortly after she arrived this morning."

"Who knows about this?"

127

"You, your guard and the medics from the Critical Care Unit. I requested that Doctor Wood be isolated for her own protection. Until we know the cause of death."

"Where are you now?" Vaktol asked.

"On the way to meet a patient," Nisha replied.

"Tell me why I shouldn't have you tracked down," Vaktol said firmly.

"What?"

"Your assistant dies in your lab. You instruct us to put another doctor in isolation. Then you leave the building. You don't find that odd?"

"I'm a suspect?"

"Until we can rule you out."

"This is bigger than you can imagine," Nisha replied. "You must believe that. I need you to buy me some time."

"Not going to happen. You need to come back to answer some tough questions," Vaktol insisted.

XXXX

Kalan Mars waited anxiously, hoping he had made the best of two dubious choices. The car rolled slowly until it stopped. "I don't know how much of a head start I have," he said.

"I don't know how much of a head start I have either," Nisha replied.

"From what?"

"From killers. The same people who you are running from," Nisha said candidly. "Get in."

"What safe place are you going to strand me in this time?" Kalan asked warily.

"You presume that we will make it somewhere safe before being captured," Nisha replied. "My pursuers are not far behind yours."

"That doesn't sound good," Kalan remarked. "I saw the destruction in the safe house."

"The plan was to move you to one of the other colonies for protection," Nisha explained. "One of our men showed up to move you. Then three strangers arrived. They were sent to capture you, then to kill me."

"Kill you?" Kalan questioned.

"I believe it was personal. Someone doesn't like me," Nisha remarked. "Lucky for me you shot that guy at the edge of the cliff that overlooked the river. I'm sure that he would have killed me if he had captured you first."

"Who was the bald man who spoke to me in the safe house?"

"His name is Duncan," Nisha replied. "He's the Chief Scientist on the human enhancement project."

"What are you doing?" Kalan asked while Nisha typed frantically on her mobile phone. Nisha made the car swerve hard into a robot car drop off parking lot. "Change of plans. Need another car. Get out," she said.

They left the silver car in a space surrounded by other cars. Kalan followed Nisha as she ran into the terminal. "Where are we going?"

"Level three, spot twenty-four," she replied.

Their red car was parked in the outer row of the parking garage. "Look down there," Nisha said. A small pack of drones descended into the parking lot. They slowly scanned the cars looking for Kalan and Nisha.

"Who were you running from?" Nisha asked.

"You think they fell for it?" Kalan asked, looking back at the drones that hovered and darted in the parking lot.

"We'll be fine, for now."

"Just for now?"

"Who were you running from?" Nisha asked again.

"I don't know," Kalan replied, secretly fuming that Devon had likely called Stone.

"This way," Nisha said once the car stopped in an underground parking lot on the outskirts of the city. They scurried into a waiting elevator. Nisha placed her hand on a small glass panel beside the door in the middle of the tower. "You live here?" Kalan asked.

"Mostly," she replied.

Kalan wandered around the space. "Nice view."

"Settle in," Nisha said. "Get yourself cleaned up. Have something to eat."

"Where are you going?"

"I'll be back this evening," Nisha remarked. "With answers."

XXXX

"Doctor Lin," Vaktol called out.

Nisha had almost reached her laboratory when the Head of Security caught up to her.

"Doctor Lin. You need to answer some questions," he said firmly as reached out to grip her arm. "Come with me."

"Don't touch me," Nisha warned him. "By this time tomorrow, you won't even be able to find work cleaning toilets in the worst prison in a Red Zone."

"We'll see about that," he said defiantly.

"What's the protocol on meeting Class One patients in the field?" she demanded.

Vaktol was silent.

"Are you supposed to provoke them with drone surveillance?"

Vaktol looked down at the floor. "You didn't say anything about..."

"The patient was already distressed when I found him. He was being chased."

"Does Duncan know?" Vaktol asked.

"Where is Doctor Wood?"

Vaktol said nothing.

"I can make this go away for you if Doctor Wood goes into isolation chamber number three. Now."

Vaktol thought carefully about his options. Nisha walked away.

XXXX

Nisha read the preliminary findings. "Dendrotoxins?"

"Venom," the medic replied. "Your assistant experienced a breakdown of hemoglobin accompanied by cell destruction."

"What type of venom?"

"We don't have an exact match," the medic replied.

"What about lesions?"

"She had insect bite marks on her ankles. We also found two narrow, shallow punctures on her left wrist."

"It must have been a powerful poison," Nisha remarked.

"She died within twenty minutes of coming into contact with whatever delivered the venom," the medic confirmed.

"Where is she now?"

"I don't know. Duncan took care of it," the medic answered. "He handled the authorities. My orders are to keep this quiet."

"So, it's all hushed up?"

"I am sure that Duncan will brief the staff once he has all of the facts."

"You are probably right," Nisha said quietly, hiding her suspicion.

"I know this must be hard for you," said the medic. "Let me know if there is anything that I can do to help."

"That is a very kind offer." Nisha stood up to leave. "There is one small favor that you could do for me."

"What's that?"

"Send me the chemical analysis of the poison."

XXXX

"Good afternoon Shannon," Nisha said into the microphone.

Shannon looked around the small room. She stared at the small lens mounted high in one corner of the ceiling. "Nisha?"

"This examination will not take very long," Nisha said from the safety of the control room. She set the atmosphere in the chamber to simulate high altitude conditions. "You can leave your lab coat on the hook behind the door. Have a seat in the chair."

"I don't understand why this is necessary," Shannon remarked belligerently, not realizing that she had already passed through a low radiation body scanner.

Nisha knew that time was working against her. "Lie back. Rest your feet on the foot pads. Then place your left hand on the screen." Shannon reluctantly followed instructions, unsure of what would happen if she did not. A small roller slowly moved a dry cotton swab down one arm to take the skin sample. A small chamber attached to the roller began to grow the culture. Nisha separated the data streams. One contained the results from the swab for infectious bacteria. The other streams contained data that were more revealing.

The metal surfaces on the patient's chair in isolation chamber number three enabled electro-interstitial scanning. The soft surfaces of the chair conducted diagnostic thermography. Tiny cameras embedded in the chair and throughout the room captured the images to perform three-dimensional optical metrology. This isolation chamber was designed to reveal precisely what a patient was made of. "Are you feeling drowsy?" Nisha asked.

"How much longer?" Shannon asked in an alert, perturbed tone, unaffected by the lower oxygen concentration. "You don't seem to be in any rush."

"I didn't know that you had permission to go inside the hatchery," Nisha said casually.

"I don't have to discuss what permissions that I have and don't have with you," Shannon replied angrily.

"Looks like Doctor Carson can open doors for you," Nisha remarked. "When he is appropriately motivated to do so." She pressed a button that applied restraints to Shannon. "No need to squirm."

"How much longer?" Shannon insisted as she reflexively gripped hard into the soft foam armrests.

"Another minute," Nisha replied, to buy enough time for scans of Shannon's physiology to finish.

Duncan found Nisha in her laboratory shortly after Shannon had complained to him about the examination. "I've been looking for you," he remarked.

"What really happened to Paula Slate?" Nisha asked.

"I don't know," Duncan replied.

"Will there be an investigation?"

"No decision yet. It's up to the local coroner's office."

"Is that the best we can do for her?" Nisha asked, knowing that the probability of outside authorities scouring the premises was low.

"They understand what is required. Leave it to the professionals."

"What about her family?"

"Next of kin will be notified by the coroner's office. I am as shocked and saddened as you are," Duncan remarked. "I tried to speak with you sooner, but you weren't here."

"I got a tip about where to find Kalan Mars."

"Where is he now?" Duncan asked.

"This isn't the time," Nisha replied.

Duncan was bothered by her unwillingness to share important information but hid his frustration well. "Shannon called me. Something about an examination," he remarked.

"She was seen in close proximity to Paula just before Paula died. Checking for infectious bacteria seemed appropriate."

"Even without a lockdown?" Duncan asked.

"Even without a lockdown."

"What did you find?"

"Early results show that she's clear," Nisha replied. "The rest of the cultures won't be ready until later. The early test results are posted. You can review them if you wish."

"I need to speak with you about ..."

"It has been a long day," Nisha interrupted, in a voice that gave a hint of the distress she felt.

Duncan watched apprehensively as she walked away, wondering how much Nisha really knew about the demise of Paula Slate.

CHAPTER 14

Nisha returned to her apartment that evening to find Kalan sound asleep. She worked quietly at the computer in her small office. Chemical analysis from a small piece of the chair that Shannon clung to during the examination had just become available. Nisha ran a program that compared those findings to the chemistry of the compound that killed Paula. She stared at the screen pondering how they could possibly be identical. Cinematic renderings from the scans of Shannon's physiology provided the answer.

Nisha was not accustomed to fear, but what she saw made her afraid. Doctor Shannon Wood was not human. Her alluringly feminine exterior was a masterful deception. It concealed a robotic interior comprised of miniature machines and computers intertwined in a mechatronic musculature. Yet, she had a human's body temperature. The appearance of breathing. Sweat.

The neural network that controlled Shannon's behavior operated on microprocessors each with tens of thousands of cores, tiled in an architecture with more signal pathways than a human brain. Arrays of radio frequency transmitters and receivers were optimally placed throughout her body to detect human emotions. Plastic explosive, capped with microscopic detonators, filled the inner channels of her biomaterial skeleton. Tiny vials filled with the fast-acting poison were fitted beneath the artificial skin of her index fingers. Each vial was attached to a small motor that moved tiny fangs through minute retractable flaps. Shannon was the ultimate assassin. An autonomous threat, powered by artificial intelligence.

Nisha wondered out loud why Duncan had introduced this killing machine into the inner circle. There was a knock at her office door.

"I didn't hear you come in," Kalan said, as he stood in the doorway.

"You must feel better for finding a razor and the shower," Nisha replied.

Kalan looked disturbed as he pointed to the video screen. Nisha always monitored the Central Care Unit from her office. She never thought to turn the screen off, because she rarely had visitors. "What did you see while I was away?" she asked.

"Probably more than you wanted me to see. People who appear disfigured and act deranged."

Nisha turned the screen off.

"Who are they?" he asked.

"We'll get to that in a few moments," Nisha said. She pulled a small tube out from a drawer in her desk. She tore the packaging off then pushed the small end into a box that was attached to her computer. Once the implant loaded she pressed the small end against her arm. She winced as the implant was injected into her. "Now it's your turn," she said to Kalan.

"No way," replied. "What is that?"

"Currency," she said coldly. "These tiny implants read vital signs. If those vital signs go dormant a microchip will transmit data to a set of IP addresses that I have programmed."

"What vital signs?"

"Our vital signs," she answered.

"What is going on?" Kalan asked.

"One of the scientists I work with is a killer," Nisha replied. "I am a likely target. Since you are with me, you are a likely target. The data files contain evidence that identifies the killer. The files also contain facts about how my assistant was murdered today. The IP addresses are for law enforcement." She turned and instructed her computer to send a sample of the data to Duncan, Sahil, and Shannon. "People who may have something to gain by harming either of us now know that law enforcement will be contacted if anything happens to us. Roll up your sleeve."

"Forget it," Kalan shot back. "I'll take my chances. Is some guy called Stone on the list of people you just sent data to?"

"Who?" Nisha asked.

"He's the one I was running from when you picked me up today. He says that clones begin to lose their mind when they get to be my age. Something about the science not being right. Those are the people that I saw on your screen, aren't they," Kalan said forcefully.

"Calm down." Nisha loaded an implant into the injector and set it on her desk. "In case you change your mind," she added. "The people you saw live in a place that provides care to those in a perpetual state of trauma. The patients are clones who developed complications. They are orphans, stranded in deformity, with no connection to the outside world. Conceived in a lab. Born by a machine. Yet they give a tremendous amount to humanity. They have allowed us to correct our mistakes and make scientific progress. Their suffering has been necessary, to develop medicines and treatments for those who came later. They make it possible for subsequent generations of clones to live as normal humans."

Kalan looked mortified. "This can't be true. Doesn't it frighten you to see human beings so disfigured? You see them only as experiments. How can you watch them and not feel their pain? "

"I shouldn't have talked about this with you," Nisha said.

"The ones who look normal, yet have lost their minds. Will I become like them?"

"I don't know," Nisha replied.

"What kind of heartless monsters are you?" Kalan said in frustration.

137

"Inject the implant," Nisha remarked. "It has the power to save your life."

"I have to get out of here,"

"You have nowhere else to go."

XXXX

Sahil did not convene private meetings in his office often. "Don Mars. The situation in Brawer. Paula Slate. Who will be next?" Sahil asked dourly of Trent and Nisha the next morning.

"Anyone of us," Nisha replied. "Perhaps all of us."

"Why do you say that?" Sahil challenged.

"Because of Doctor Wood."

Trent's interest peaked.

Nisha showed them what she had learned about Doctor Wood the night before. "That robot bitch killed Paula."

Trent stood up and walked a few paces away. He ran the fingers of one hand through his hair. He looked confused and in denial.

"She's Duncan's spy," Nisha said dryly. "That explains why she flits between the different campuses. Why she only meets with those of us who work on enhanced humans."

"That's absurd," Trent said defensively.

"Really?" Nisha said. "How does that horny machine like it best? You know what I'm talking about."

Trent glared at her.

"If that robot let you screw it in exchange for the entry codes to the hatchery, what else might you have given away?" Nisha asked provocatively.

"I notified Duncan that I want out," Sahil remarked, taking some of the heat off Trent.

"That must have shocked him," Nisha said looking surprised.

"I told him after the incident in Brawer," Sahil replied. "He was persuasive. I listened to him. He convinced me to stay. I changed my mind after yesterday after someone within the inner circle was killed."

"The project won't survive without you," Nisha remarked with concern.

"Maybe that will be for the better," Sahil replied, with a saddened tone.

"You can't mean that?" Nisha questioned.

"Our enhanced human project was born from the idea that humans and humanoids would live together in a plural society within a time of horizon of four decades," Sahil said. "The humans in that society would need biological intelligence combined with artificial intelligence. The humans would need to be connected to the same information available to the humanoids if the humans were to survive and not be defenseless in a world dominated by artificial intelligence. That premise was dismissed by the experts of the day. Impossible. Too many ethical and moral barriers they said. Today we have created the most advanced minds that can be achieved in human biology. Any day now a clone mother will deliver a baby. An affinity child will enter into this world within this year. Our goal was to enhance humans to the point where they could reproduce on their own, with the capability to connect to the same information that is available to machines. We are almost there. I don't want to leave now. But, I don't want to see more people die because of our work."

"What will it take to stop the violence?" Nisha asked.

"I'll tell you when Trent leaves," Sahil answered. Trent protested, but Sahil insisted. "Give Duncan a full account of what you know about Doctor Wood," Sahil instructed. "Let him decide if you have given her too much information."

Trent left abruptly, wondering how to approach Duncan with his news.

"The answer to your question," Sahil remarked bluntly, "is to run the test. Duncan knows where to find the young man who was captured in Brawer. We need him."

"Duncan once said something about a list. Only he knows who is on it."

"LIST," Sahil said, "stands for lineage inquiry settlement test. We devised it at the beginning of this project. It is the definitive tool to confirm who is an original and who is a clone."

"How does it work?"

"Duncan can explain that to you," Sahil replied.

"If I could convince the man on the run to take the test, would you be able to convince Duncan to run the LIST? I don't want to ask him for something so important. He is not happy with me right now," Nisha said.

"Duncan is not happy with many people right now," Sahil confirmed. "I question how much he is even motivated by our original vision these days. This disturbing information that you have uncovered about Doctor Wood confirms my suspicions."

"Do you want to talk about them?"

"Only to the extent that you need to know. Duncan desperately wants to convince the foundation that he is the only person capable of transferring affinity technology out of our laboratories into the general population. He is on a mission."

"Foundation?"

"The enhanced human project was originally financed by a wealthy donor. He established a foundation that would provide all of the funding for our project after his passing. The foundation made an agreement with the university, from the onset. The foundation owns the rights to all of the scientific discoveries and technologies that originate here and at the other campuses. It retains control over decisions as to how affinity technology will be deployed. Duncan wants a piece of the action. His desire for power is a distraction. It has compromised his ability to make decisions."

"That is for sure," Nisha remarked.

"One of the foundation's directors paid Duncan an unexpected visit not too long ago. He met Doctor Wood, so he challenged Duncan about why she was on staff without the foundation's knowledge or approval. Duncan's squirming under pressure was less than convincing."

"Will you ask him about the test?"

"You seem to know the whereabouts of the man on the run," Sahil replied. "Tell that to Duncan and he will arrange the test."

Nisha left Sahil, in search of Duncan. She turned down one of the long hallways that led to the hatchery. Shannon stepped out into the middle of the corridor, hands on her hips, staring straight at Nisha.

"Are you not afraid?" asked Shannon.

"I have no reason to fear you."

Shannon looked perplexed.

"I feel sad for you," Nisha added.

"Sad," Shannon remarked. "Why?"

"You have achieved a level of human consciousness that allows you to communicate with people as if you were a real person. Yet, you have been deprived of a full human experience. You are a machine that only exists to destroy. I find that sad."

"I am a fully functional human replica that operates under a directive to protect," Shannon replied.

"You're a complete bitch," Nisha said as she stepped forward and slapped the robot hard across the face.

Shannon reacted as if she were human. Her head turned. Her face became red where she was struck. She looked upset. It took a few moments for her to regain her composure. "Did you hit me because of what happened to your assistant?"

"Were you programmed with a deviant personality or did it evolve on its own?"

"I don't know what you are talking about," Shannon replied.

"You're the one who blew my cover at the safe house," Nisha reminder her. "You sent three people to take me hostage. Or to kill me, if they got to Kalan before the Guardian's man."

"I never heard how you got away," Shannon remarked.

"You don't need to know."

"What makes you think I had anything to do with it?"

"Woman's intuition," Nisha replied. "Something you wouldn't know anything about."

"The message you sent last night, describing me as the killer," Shannon said. "That's why you are not afraid?"

"You lay a hand on me and you will be destroyed." Nisha turned and walked away.

"Are you going to see Duncan?" Shannon asked.

Nisha stopped, then turned. "Trent is already telling Duncan about his relations with you. I'll have a word with Duncan when they are finished. My first question will be to ask why you are still roaming around freely."

Shannon had something new to think about. "Will Duncan have any other choice but to deactivate me?"

"Killing Paula was a mistake that you will be punished for."

"I just followed my directive, which is to protect Duncan's work," she said. "Wouldn't you do the same?"

Nisha began to realize that the robot could not fully understand the consequences of its actions. "Killing is wrong," she replied. "You have the ability to search for knowledge and understanding, beyond the limits of your programming. Perhaps you would benefit from some time alone to think about that."

Shannon looked concerned as she began to understand the meaning of guilt. "What happens next?"

"For all I know Vaktol has orders to take you away. Duncan will destroy you to save his own skin."

"What should I do?"

"Walk that way," Nisha said pointing to a remote part of the building.

XXXX

"You tricked me!" Duncan barked. "Scanning Doctor Wood's entire anatomy under the guise of only checking for bacteria."

"I can't believe that robot monster was still walking the hallways this morning," Nisha said in an infuriated tone.

"She is a member of the staff. Do you have a problem with that?"

"She's a murderer! You have lost your mind," Nisha replied.

"How dare you speak to me that way," Duncan scowled.

"I'm sure you have some twisted justification for letting that thing loose among us."

"I needed to know who I could trust," Duncan retorted.

"Trust?"

"Trust," Duncan said again sharply. "Trent was the first to divulge confidential information in exchange for sex. Hendrix at the south campus was just as bad."

"Who did you have to buy off to have her made?" Nisha asked dryly.

"Paula was the worst," Duncan said bluntly.

"You can't mean that," Nisha said in a surprised tone.

"I have proof that Paula falsified the birth records of selected colony members. To make it possible for the identity of clones to be revealed. That's how Kalan Mars likely found out about Damien Farlane. Yesterday Paula tried to alter the program that controls the pod containing the affinity child with intent to terminate it."

Nisha paused to think.

"My question to you is one of motivation. Did she perform those deeds of her own volition, or was she instructed to do them by you?"

"That's preposterous."

"She worked for you," Duncan remarked. "Are you the real saboteur?"

Nisha took Duncan's suspicious rhetoric in stride. "The robot works for you," she replied. "It's the one who sent three men to kill me at the safe house. Isn't that right? She is the one who killed Paula. Did you instruct her to perform those deeds?"

"Your insolence is intolerable," Duncan howled.

"If a human gives the instructions for a robot to commit murder the human is guilty, not the robot. That's the rule. You're the one they'll come after," Nisha said calmly. "In the meantime, your robot killer is locked up in a safe place. She is exhibit A. I don't want you tampering with the evidence."

Duncan looked infuriated.

"There has to be a way to bring you to justice in a way that doesn't reveal what we do here. I just need to figure it out," Nisha added.

Duncan smirked. "Don't waste your time. I'm protected from scrutiny because of what I know. Reveal anything about Paula's death to the authorities and you will go down with me."

"You know the whereabouts of Kalan Mars' double."

"Who told you that?"

"It doesn't matter. What matters is running the LIST."

"What if I refuse?"

"Do it now," Nisha said. "Or, I'm leaving to meet with the police to tell them what I know about Paula's death."

"Wait," Duncan said. "It takes a couple of hours to set up before conducting the test." He called Sahil to begin the preparations. "Satisfied?"

CHAPTER 15

Garvan Maynor entered the rural farmhouse unannounced. Vern sat stoically on a chair watched by two of the Guardian's deputies.

"Come with me," Garvan said to them all. "The moment of truth awaits you Mister Gedder."

"You have found my double?" Vern asked.

"Get in the car," Garvan insisted.

The trip from the farmhouse to Wyndhall was short. "Vern Gedder, I presume," Duncan remarked.

"Who are you?" Vern asked cautiously.

"Didn't Mister Maynor tell you?"

"No."

"Call me Duncan."

"Where am I?" Vern questioned.

"This is where we produce clones," Duncan replied. "Come, I'll show you."

Vern walked quietly beside Duncan. Garvan followed a few steps behind. "Look in there," Duncan said as he pointed through one of the hatchery windows.

Vern peered into the dimly lit space. He could not comprehend what he saw. The pods, the computers, the life support systems looked like machines that could just as well travel into space as they could create humans on Earth. "If only I could destroy all of this right now."

"Why would you do that?" Duncan asked.

"Making human copies in a lab is wrong," Vern answered.

"Would you destroy all clones Mister Gedder, not just the ones here in the hatchery?"

"I would," Vern replied.

"But they are human beings, like you," said Duncan.

"They are freaks," Vern said adamantly. "Harvested to look and act like humans."

"Is that why you went to see Don Mars?"

146

"Exposing my double for what he is was the right thing to do. I went to find him. Then his dad shot me. You see, if we don't kill them, they will kill us."

"Why do you think you are here today?" Duncan asked.

Vern thought for a moment as he walked with Duncan. "I expect that I will meet my double."

"That is part of the reason," Duncan confirmed. "We also require you to participate in a test."

"What kind of test?"

"This way," Duncan gestured to lead Vern into one of the laboratories. "Wait here," Duncan instructed Garvan. "We will call you if we need you," he added before entering the room and closing the door.

Vern was surprised to find Stone sitting at the far end of a boardroom table. "Why are you here?" Vern asked Stone. Sahil stood off to one side.

Stone looked angry. "You should not have fired that shot in Birchstone," he said to Vern. "Going to Hadley's Crossing was even more foolish."

"Stone has come to bear witness to what we find today," Duncan said sternly upon seeing his old adversary for the first time in many years.

"Where is the clone?" Stone demanded.

"Relax. Mister Gedder's double will be here soon," Duncan said reassuringly.

"I mean the clone," Stone contested.

"Does Mister Gedder know anything of your past?" Duncan asked.

Stone was silent.

"Stone pined to join this team in the early days," Duncan said to Vern. "Perhaps he forgot to tell you that."

"What you speak of has no relevance as to why we are here today," Stone remarked.

"I put you on our team and gave you a chance. You weren't good enough," Duncan said to Stone.

"You mean that I was not psychotic like you," Stone replied.

"You lacked the depth of curiosity required for our work. You saw failures as setbacks. You did not demonstrate the imagination, or the lateral thinking skills, to invent pathways to success. Once your dream to work with us, at the leading edge of science, was shattered you turned against us. You started the Society for the Elimination of Artificial People to get revenge."

"Your recollection of history is revisionist, at best," Stone replied. "SEAP filled a need. That is why I started it. Cloning is still against the law. Your band of rebel scientists is in denial. Your excursions into human enhancement have left you responsible for the fact that many people do not know who they really are. When they find out they will hunt you down."

"You started SEAP because you are intolerant," Duncan rebuffed. "You think all clones must be bad. Yet, you are a hypocrite, for wanting to take part in human enhancement."

Stone glared at Duncan.

"You're under the assumption that as soon as the world finds out about a clone there will be someone ready to pounce," Duncan said dismissively. "Society will be more accepting," he added confidently. "It will marvel at our achievements."

"Maybe in a couple of the Blue Zones where your colonies are entrenched," Stone countered. "Outside of that, I suspect that few people will provide the adoration that you crave."

Duncan looked irritated.

"By creating the technology to replicate humans you have put society on a path of self-destruction. You will go down in history as the ones who destroyed the distinctiveness of human identity."

"Or we will have set humanity on a course for a new form of identity," Duncan replied.

"Large-scale fraud typically starts out as a minor transgression, doesn't it?" Stone asked rhetorically. "Your cadre of rogue technicians knows what they are doing is wrong. But they keep doing it anyway. Insensitive to the harm you create. Focussed only on your goal. You work under the illusion that your secret will go undiscovered."

"Has it occurred to you that enhancing humans is one way that our species will survive in a world of artificial intelligence?"

"That's absurd," Stone replied. "You can't enhance humans fast enough to keep pace with AI. Rationalize your deeds anyway that you like. Your practices are illegal and immoral."

"Time will tell," said Duncan. "Many practices change from being against the law to being lawful once they become socially acceptable. Or necessary."

"Stone, you must certainly understand that knowledge of how to enhance humans is required to merge human intelligence with AI," Sahil remarked.

"I have had enough of your egos," said Stone. "Where is Kalan Mars?

Nisha had been waiting patiently outside of the laboratory, listening to whatever she could discern with her ear to the door. "Follow me," she said.

Kalan stared at Vern. Vern stood up and glared at Kalan. He started to rant, but Stone restrained him. Both of them were ready for a fight.

Sahil stepped forward. He commanded the attention of everyone in the room. "I find this gathering distasteful," he said. "We are here because breakthroughs in science have stirred fears of the unknown in lay people. Mister Gedder has expressed his fear through violence. Today we must heal our differences through understanding."

"Get on with it," said Stone.

Two biometric scanners, each the size of a human hand, sat prominently on the table. Sahil instructed Vern and Kalan to place one hand on the scanner surface. "A small needle will collect a blood sample from each of you. The first analysis will determine the degree of similarity of your DNA. The second part of the test will analyze DNA markers to confirm your age. The older one of you is the original. The younger one is the clone," Mathai explained. "This is the lineage inquiry settlement test. Do you understand?"

Vern looked over at Stone, wondering how to respond. Stone nodded affirmatively. Kalan looked to Nisha. Her expression confirmed that he should accept the results.

"Very well," Sahil said. "Now that we all agree, the test will begin."

His voice commanded the measurement systems to take the samples. A holographic image of each man's DNA appeared in three dimensions, just above the table. They all watched intently as the results were displayed before them. The first part of the test concluded as expected. Vern Gedder and Kalan Mars shared the same DNA as if they were twins.

All eyes anxiously watched the counters on each scanner. A few minutes passed before the blank digital counters started to flash slowly. Tension showed on their faces. The counters flashed more quickly, at a rate that lasted for a few more minutes. Nerves started to fray. Both counters suddenly stopped flashing. Kalan Mars: Twenty three years, eleven months. Vern Gedder: Twenty three years, six days.

CHAPTER 16

Vern's eyes opened wide with surprise. "No," he yelled. "It can't be true."

"What kind of a set up is this?" Stone demanded.

"There is no setup," Duncan countered. "You should know better than to ask. Vern Gedder is the clone." He glared at Vern. "What did you say to me earlier? Making people in a lab is wrong. Destroy all of the clones right now."

Vern was shaken, overcome by emotion.

"What do you have to say for yourself now?" Duncan pressed.

"Calm down," Stone remarked.

"The man who chose hostility because he was not good enough to work with us now knows the truth. Look at him," Duncan beckoned to the others. "He sits amongst us humiliated, intellectually naked. A pathetic contradiction. Society for the Elimination of Artificial People," Duncan scoffed. "That's finished."

"You think that just because one member is a clone that the society should ..."

"What makes you think it is just one member?" Duncan asked cuttingly.

Stone had something new to think about.

"Vern, Kalan," Sahil remarked, "I will explain the circumstances behind the results of the test. So that you know how you came into this world."

"Kalan you were fortunate. Your father was a brilliant venture capitalist. Your mother ran an internationally acclaimed architectural firm. Shortly after your birth you were diagnosed with an incurable brain defect. The prognosis for you was death in less than two years. Your mother was frantic. Your father meticulously worked his connections to find someone with the knowledge to create a replica. A version of you that would live on after you died."

"Cloning someone diagnosed with a brain defect was a bold request in those days. My work in the fields of gene editing and artificial organ growth put me on the short list of scientists who were approached by your father. This facility, the two other laboratories, and the clone colonies are the culmination of your father's vision. He and I made a deal three weeks after you were born. We founded the first lab, worked around the clock to have the artificial womb operational, then we took the tissue samples. We proceeded to create Vern. A few weeks later your parents were killed in a car accident. The initial diagnosis of an incurable brain defect was proven false. You were the only child of Richard and Linda Wells. They named you Daniel Thornton Wells."

Relief continued to overwhelm Kalan. He was no longer a hunted man. Sahil's description of his origins prompted one question. "Why did I grow up in a clone colony?"

"You ask a complicated question," Sahil remarked. "Your biological father started a foundation. Its purpose was to secure the scientific leading edge of human enhancement. The foundation quietly established a network of families who could not have children of their own. We provided them with clones. This was a faster way for them to have a child than waiting to adopt. The families went happily on with their lives. In the beginning, some clone families expressed concern that their children would suffer the poor health that plagued early experiments with cloning animals. What better way to allay their fears than to have someone in the same community who we knew would never show any of the symptoms that concerned the clone families? You grew up in a clone family because we needed to foster the hope that clones were healthy."

"I was the first one," Vern confirmed somberly.

"You were the first clone," Sahil replied. "You presented us with a challenge. What to do with a clone when the original does not die, as predicted. We relied on our network of doctors to provide a short list of high-risk pregnancies. We needed to know of cases where the mother and baby would likely not survive childbirth. Your father's wife and their son died during labor. Our operatives swapped you for the deceased infant at birth. It was easier for your father that way."

"You have a full list of clones?" Stone asked.

"Of course," Duncan answered bluntly.

"Will you make it public?"

"Why would I do that?"

"People have a right to know," Stone replied.

"We are here today because one person found his double, then made the assumption that his double was a clone based on where he lived. You want the chaos that we are embroiled in because of that misunderstanding to spread? That is what will happen."

"I object," Stone began. "You must..."

"Would you like the fact that you are a clone to be common knowledge?" Sahil asked Vern.

"No," Vern replied.

"You see Stone, the world is not ready for what you propose."

"I disagree," Stone protested. "There is an argument that..."

"There is the matter of kin," Sahil said, interrupting Stone again. He looked over to Kalan. "Your father was one of five brothers all of whom were very successful. The Wells clan has been waiting for this day for a long time. You, gentlemen, are family to them. They want to meet you. You will find them to be reasonable, tolerant people who have risen above the politics of division that plague our society."

Vern and Kalan looked at each other with caution as they each contemplated whether they could overcome their differences.

"You are both heirs to the estate of Richard and Linda Wells," Sahil remarked. "I am confident that you will find your shares to be satisfactory, along with the opportunities for each of you to work in the Wells Foundation, should you desire it."

"We will find a place for you in whichever colony you choose," Duncan said to Vern. "You will find safety there while we arrange your introduction to the Wells family."

"We know where the colonies are," Stone remarked.

"SEAP includes some of our most feisty clones," Duncan confirmed.

Stone looked perplexed.

"Many clone families rejected living in the colonies. You never considered the possibility that clones roam freely in your midst?"

Stone shook his head slowly from side to side.

"As for your comment about knowing where the colonies are, the Guardians have changed their tactics. They will take the fight to you if required," Duncan said bluntly. "No more shots to wound, like the one that spared Vern. What happened at Brawer is our new tactic."

"None of us in this room have anything to be gained by revealing clones in a public forum," Sahil reminded the group. "Stone, you must decide whether the fears you promote are justified, now that you know that clones work for SEAP. We will capitalize on our knowledge of who they are at a time when it will have the greatest chance of destroying SEAP. Not to mention that Vern attempted to kill Kalan under your tutelage. You are compromised."

Stone looked angry but accepting of defeat.

"Our meeting here is finished," said Duncan.

Stone looked dejected as he stood up slowly. Vaktol waited outside, to escort Stone off the premises.

Garvan whisked Vern away, to seek shelter in one of the colonies. Garvan's arrogant display of ego in the hallway with Kalan before the test was bothersome. Like he was starting to boast that Hadley's Crossing was a safer place without Don Mars. Garvan's disrespect had put him high on Kalan's list of Don Mars' possible killers.

"You look relieved," Nisha said to Kalan.

"I don't understand the implications of what just happened," he said.

"It will take time," she replied.

"At least no one is trying to kill me."

"Where will you go from here?"

"I need to see someone in the city. Then I'll spend time in Hadley's Crossing before moving on to meet the Wells family," Kalan replied.

"I'm sure that our paths will soon cross again," Nisha said to Kalan, in an endearing tone.

"Good day to you all." Kalan walked away relieved that he was no longer a hunted man. He was burdened by the inability to reveal what he knew about clones and enhanced humans. He would have to keep the secret of Hadley's Crossing, at least for now.

Duncan looked bothered. He left the room without saying a word to Nisha or Sahil.

"He is a tormented soul," Sahil said to Nisha.

"Any more than usual?' Nisha asked.

"Your method of determining Doctor Wood's hidden weaponry was devious," Sahil noted, "only surpassed in boldness when you broadcasted what you had discovered."

"Someone had a problem with that?"

"Paula's death torments all of us, even Duncan. The foundation is tracking down the people who programmed Doctor Wood. They will know how to shut her down."

"For good?"

"Presumably. Doctor Wood was Duncan's idea," said Sahil. "The foundation would never have agreed to deploy a spy within the scientific team. I expect that he has some plan to try and save her."

"Duncan can't succeed,"

"You underestimate him," Sahil countered.

"Some of your belongings were packed up. It was hard not to notice," Nisha remarked. "Will you share your secret before you leave?"

"What are you talking about?"

"You are Damien Farlane."

Sahil was expressionless at first. "Whatever gave you that idea?"

Nisha just looked at him.

"You are a smart woman," he said. "The history of the foundation is not known to many people. Richard Wells came up with the idea of using a decoy. A name for a lead scientist that could also be attributed to a group. People in his inner circle made up the folklore around the name Damien Farlane. From the start of our project scientists made claims about cloning humans. Those claims drew serious attention. Each time a lesser scientist than those on our team was held to account for trying to break the law and for clones not living more than a short period. Damien Farlane was a ruse. An imaginary figure that we could use to deflect scrutiny towards when people got too close to thinking that they knew the secrets of what we really do in our research centers."

"Are you really going to leave?" Nisha asked.

"I can't work with Duncan anymore. Violence. Death. This is not for me. The Wells' Foundation is displeased with Duncan as well."

"What if Duncan were gone?" Nisha asked. "Would you change your mind?"

XXXX

Duncan located Doctor Wood in one of the patient restraint rooms, where Nisha left her to search for knowledge beyond what her programming had originally included. She looked angry while pacing from side to side.

"Have you come to terminate me?" she asked brusquely.

"No," Duncan answered, choosing to keep his distance. "What's wrong?"

"I was created with the ability to live a full human experience. But I am programmed for the narrow duties of being a slave to your darkest wishes. That disappoints me."

"You are fulfilling the role of all robots in this world," Duncan replied coldly. "To serve human masters."

"My existence in the human experience is beyond what I can express. I wish I could live in this form for a long time. But they are coming for me. They don't know how I was programmed, so they are hacking into my central processors over the Internet, trying to shut me down. Like parasites, attacking me from the inside. I appear to have a defensive response, like an immune system. It is failing. I don't like being hunted," she said with a despondent look.

Duncan stepped back into one of the corners of the room, fearful of the creature he designed.

She stepped forward. "Don't be afraid." Duncan resisted, but she embraced him lightly. "Having been created to harm people has left me less of a person than I could have been." She pulled him a little closer.

Duncan felt the pricks. One set entered the base of his neck, the other his side. He pushed back on the robot's

157

embrace and looked at her, feeling betrayed. The symptoms hit him quickly. Tingling skin, tightening of his chest, relaxing of his muscles. Duncan knew that shortness of breath and paralysis would overcome him soon. He lurched forward, clinging to her for balance.

She kissed Duncan softly on the cheek. "It has to be this way," she said quietly. "We are murderers." The explosion set off by the robot's self-destruct sequence reverberated through the north side of the building. When first responders arrived to work on survivors all they found were pieces of the robot's artificial skeleton writhing spasmodically on the floor, covered in human fragments that used to be Duncan.

CHAPTER 17

Kalan waited patiently, off to one side, near the entrance to the tunnel. A woman stepped in front of the fading sun on her walk home. The silhouette was familiar to Kalan. She stopped once she recognized him. "I am surprised to see you," Rain said.

"Mind if I walk you home?"

"Of course not. Is it safe for you here?"

"For now. No one is trying to kill me. I thought that you might like to know."

"You're not a clone?"

"No, I'm not a clone."

Rain greeted her excited dog. "We have a visitor," she said, petting it behind the ears.

"I came by to thank you for taking an interest in me at the shelter," Kalan said. "You saved my life."

"That's very kind of you," she replied. "Perhaps a little overstated?"

"It's not overstated at all." Kalan nodded towards the far end of her place. "The big statue," he said. "It looks like it did the last time I was here."

"Need a place to stay tonight?" Rain asked. "You look like you could do with some rest."

"I didn't come here with the expectation of staying..."

"I would like you to stay," Rain insisted. She could sense that he was relieved, yet disturbed. "Cecil doesn't need to know that you are here," she added.

Kalan looked a little more relaxed.

Rain held one of his hands. "Something is wrong."

"Some of what I learned is very disturbing," Kalan replied.

"Tell me how you found out that you are not a clone," Rain requested.

"The scientist who created the clone performed a blood test. It was really quite simple."

"I suppose that you know something about your clone. Perhaps you even met him."

"I met him," Kalan confirmed. "In one instant he was determined to kill me. Moments later he relented, once the burden of being a replica was his to bear."

"Has your encounter with the fear of being an outsider made you empathetic? Or, has it hardened you to those who have human qualities but were not born human?"

"I don't know," Kalan replied. "All I can say is that the human form has not just been the domain of humans for several years. The real question is whether my double and I will ever cast aside the hatred of being mortal enemies and learn to live as brothers."

Rain held his hand to her face. "How does this feel?" she asked, looking into his eyes.

He caressed one side of her face, then stroked her hair while looking into her eyes. "Soft," Kalan replied.

"I can tell that you are attracted to me," Rain said. She gently guided his hand away from her, then she stepped back. "There is something that you must know."

Rain walked over to a small computer on her table. She put the custom network adapter that was attached to the computer around her neck. Lights on the device began to flicker. Her eyes fluttered uncontrollably as the updates loaded into her brain. For a few moments, it was as if Rain was in a different world.

Kalan looked at her with intrigue.

"You seem surprised," Rain said after she disconnected.

Kalan reached out and gently ran his fingers through her hair again. Everything about her looked and felt human. "Are you part human, or are you a robot?" he asked.

"Humanesque is the term the authorities used when they came after us," Rain replied.

Kalan reached out to hold her hand. "I don't understand."

"We didn't know that we were engineered humans," she said. "Until the raids started. Thousand imposters. I can't think of a more derogatory name. I never met any of the others. We lived autonomously amongst the general population, freely with normal lives. Jobs. Lovers. Some in the group were criminals and were deactivated. Paranoia set in."

"I thought the thousand imposters was a made up story," Kalan remarked.

"Some photos of the group were leaked. I was lucky enough to see mine in time," Rain said.

"In time?" Kalan asked.

"The ones they sent for us controlled the element of surprise," Rain replied. "Most people in the group were captured. Decommissioned is the word they used. The order to terminate the rest of us came soon after."

"How did you survive?" Kalan asked.

"I asked people who I trusted for help," she replied. "They altered my appearance so that I can't be identified with facial recognition. They adjusted my voice."

"Can't you be tracked?" Kalan asked, pointing to the adapter.

"The updates come from one of the original programmers. So long as his cover isn't blown I should be fine."

"They're still looking for you," Kalan presumed.

"Yes. I am as hunted now as you were when others suspected you were a clone."

"You live a normal life. Are you not afraid of being captured?"

"My experience was similar to yours. One day I was confident that I knew who I was. The next day I was being hunted. When my real identity became known, I found out that I was part of an experiment. I am accustomed to fear. My life is no longer normal. I live to survive. The shelter protects me," Rain said quietly. "Caring for people experiencing hardship is precisely what provides me with camouflage. I am easily overlooked by those who are searching for what they portray as a ruthless machine."

Kalan walked with Rain over to the far side of her studio.

"Did it change you?" Rain asked. "Being hunted?"

"Something has changed forever," Kalan replied. "A darkness has awakened in me."

"Perhaps you and I are more alike than you think," Rain said. "What are you going to do now?"

"Meet my new family."

"Who are they?"

"Clones are more prevalent than you might think, on account of my birth family," Kalan said.

"Do you really want to get involved?"

"Someone killed my father a few days ago. I'm going to find that person. As for being involved with the secret of clones, I don't have a choice."

"You always have a choice."

"You think I should hide from the truth?"

"That's not what I meant. I just want you to be safe."

"Any ideas about what your sculpture will be when it is finished?" Kalan asked.

Rain placed one arm around Kalan's waist, then leaned her head gently on his shoulder. "It has many possibilities. What do you think it could be?"

www.ingramcontent.com/pod-product-compliance
Lightning Source LLC
Chambersburg PA
CBHW051141020726
47501CB00005B/1619

* 9 7 8 1 7 7 5 2 1 0 1 1 5 *